Kit Wilson, RN:
First Year Nurse

Beth E. Heinzeroth White

IBSN number:
978-1-735-9347-0-9 (paperback)
978-1-735-9347-1-6 (digital/e-book)

This book is a work of fiction. Any resemblance to locations or persons, living or dead, is a coincidence. The story is purely from my imagination and
not a reflection of any actual events. This book is not meant to be a medical
or nursing reference. The author has made every effort to ensure that the
information in this book was correct at the publication date.

First printing edition 2022
BHW Publishing
Permissions address:
Bethewhite.09@gmail.com

This book is dedicated to:

o   The millions of nurses who every day and night willingly negotiate our baffling health care system to provide compassionate, knowledgeable care to patients and families. You are the scaffolding that supports health care. Without you, hospitals simply would have no reason to exist.

o   Emily, Nora, and Elliott, Colleen, Teddy, Lucy, and Poppy. They call me Mom and Grandma Bethie and are my most important fans.

o   Lee R. Lake, biomedical engineer extraordinaire. Kit would not be possible without your original idea and encouragement.

Contents

Acknowledgments

o The readers who reviewed multiple revisions to this book are acknowledged with gratitude. Your edits were frequently insightful and often brilliant. Thank you from the bottom of my heart: Barbara Keith; Beth Wilhelm; Cassie Zak; Nora Klepacz; Erin Czerniak; Judy Szor; Julie Beitelschiess; Kevin Hayes; Lee Lake; Maria Nowicki; Maureen Knowles; Norma Lake; Patricia Ringos Beach; Sue Eisel; Susan Breckinridge; Vicki Koelsch; Yarko Kuk.

o Credit is given to many nursing scholars for explaining and making sense of what nursing is. Those directly referenced in this book are referenced here:

   o Patricia Benner. (1984) Novice to Expert: Excellence and Power in Clinical Practice. Hoboken, NJ: Prentice-Hall Publishers.

   o Dorthea Orem. (1971) An American nursing theorist who has developed a nursing theory known as Orem's Self Care Deficit Theory, based on the individual's ability to perform self-care on their own behalf in maintaining life, health, and well-being.

   o Jean Watson. (1979) An American nursing theorist. Jean Watson's Nursing Theory of Human Caring.

o Jonelle Massey. (2021) The Miseducation of Empathy. Toledo, Ohio: Jane Mae Publishing.

o Special acknowledgment goes to Florence Nightingale (1820-1910), often considered the founder of modern nursing. Some of her quotes, which continue to resonate in nursing practice, are found at the beginning of each chapter.

o *Annie's Song*. (1974) John Denver, composer, and performer. In the album Back Home Again, Milt Okun, producer.

o *In-a-Godda-Da-Vita*. (1968) Doug Ingle, composer. Performed by Iron Butterfly. In the album, In-a-Gadda-Da-Vita, Jim Hilton, producer.

o *Freedom*. (1969) performed by Richie Havens. In the album Freedom at Woodstock. Based on traditional spiritual Motherless Child.

o *Love is a Many Splendored Thing*. (1955) Sammy Fain and Paul Francis Webster, composers.

o Professional nursing refers to a registered nurse. At the time of publication, there are three ways to enter professional nursing. An Associate of Science in Nursing (ASN) degree route takes approximately two years, a diploma route takes about three years, and a Bachelor of Science in Nursing (BSN) degree route takes approximately four years. Each program will allow the successful graduate to sit for the national licensing exam NCLEX (National Council Licensure Examination). Successful completion of NCLEX is required by each state in the United States to be designated as a registered nurse.

Prologue

<u>Our first journey is to find that special place for us.</u>
<u>Florence Nightingale.</u>

I have a deep blue T-Shirt that proclaims Protector, Warrior, Hero, <u>Nurse</u>. A grateful family member gave it to me during the peak of the 2020-2021 Covid 19 pandemic. The shirt fitted like a glove and was locally made. It feels humbling to be called a warrior and hero and a little self-aggrandizing to wear it emblazoned right below my masked face.

The T-shirt has had quite an effect. When wearing it, I've received countless observations about nursing, and in almost every comment, the person imagined what it must be like to be a nurse. Quotes ranging from, "Oh, I could never be a nurse. The things you have to do! Blech!" and "You're a saint." or, "I have always wanted to be a nurse. I'm a caring person, and I like to help people," and two of my favorites, "Do you really have to go to college to be a nurse?" and "What's it really like to be a nurse?"

I think that it's incredibly common for people to be curious about nursing. Everyone has had some encounter with a nurse. We're a big group. Did you ever think that hospitals would have no reason to exist if it wasn't for the need for nurses? Really. You can get surgery, physician evaluation, medications, lab tests, and X-Rays outside a hospital. It's when you need a nurse to monitor your health around the clock that you need to stay in a hospital.

You may already know that nursing is widely considered a distinguished, almost sacred profession. For over 20 years, the general public has identified nursing as the "most trusted profession" in Gallup polls. Nurses receive the top ranking for their honesty and ethical standards. That makes me feel proud to be a nurse. But public opinion doesn't tell you what it's like to be a nurse.

My name is Catherine Wilson, but almost everyone calls me Kit. I've been practicing nursing for over four years, and it's still a long way before I'm considered an expert nurse. Nurses don't move from novice to expert nurse on a straight path. I'm a nurse, and I'd love to tell you some stories about how my first year as a registered nurse began the work of developing me from a beginning first-year novice into a competent registered nurse.

I graduated from Trail State University (TSU) in 2018 with a Bachelor of Science in Nursing. (Just to clarify, yes, you do have to go to college to be a nurse.) TSU is huge and sits on the outskirts of the county seat. The College of Nursing and the Medical School have excellent reputations. We sit in the middle of the United States, Fly Over Country for those who live on the coasts. Since graduation, almost four years ago, I've worked in a medium-sized hospital in the community where I was born and raised. It's called Thompson Memorial Hospital (TMH) and is 120 miles from TSU. My hospital is part of the more extensive TSU health care system, of which TSU hospital is the clinical centerpiece. Because the TSU health system is progressive, new nurses participate in an intensive mentored six-month orientation. It's called the nurse residency program and is how I started my journey as a registered nurse.

So. What's nursing really like? Let me tell you what it's like from my perspective.

Why would a person want to be a nurse? Here is the truth. Nursing is physically and emotionally, and cognitively a hard knock life. No sane person has ever said they want to be a nurse because they crave being with people who are violent when they are not oriented, who can't control their bowels or bladders, who refuse to break habits that have the potential to kill them early like smoking, overeating, or overindulging in alcohol, and those who are dying. In addition, no one (who has a lick of financial sense anyway) goes into nursing for the money.

That is not to say that nursing can't be a satisfying profession. In my experience, nursing can be fulfilling, intellectually challenging, and personally affirming.

You don't have to be a nurse to have a sense of what nurses do. There are patterns and experiences frequently shared by all nurses. A lot of these are almost universal experiences in life. Nursing stories are about humans struggling with familiar tough issues.

Nurses see more of these situations more frequently than most people. This frequency of exposure is a two-edged sword, making nurses more compassionate, relatable, and effective. As you'll find out in the story of my first year, it can have the effect of making nurses more case-hardened, even cynical.

The first year of professional nursing practice is a distinct time. In the first year of practice, every nurse comes face to face with heightened responsibilities, multiple technical skills that must be performed safely, and team skills to learn. Probably the biggest test for new nurses is developing a system of organizing tasks and their time. Setting priorities when there are multiple demands on a nurse's attention is essential and a huge challenge for new nurses. Getting stuff done is not even the trickiest part. A nurse's organizational skills must include proficiency with the unique underpinnings in nursing: caring, compassion, empathy, respect for everyone's dignity, and an astute understanding of what is happening in a situation.

The road to competency is so uneven and unpredictable that practically every first-year nurse says they feel like an imposter sometimes. It took me quite a while to stop wondering how the heck the hospital could leave me in charge of these sick people. I didn't feel like I knew what the devil I was doing. I often felt that what they taught me in school had nothing to do with what I needed to know to be a good hospital nurse. Sometimes I felt sure many of the other nurses in the hospital knew I was too stupid ever to be a competent nurse, and they were just tolerating me until I realized it and moved on. Frankly, I also learned from experienced nurses who helped me become a safe RN through patience and firm but kind direction.

The first year of nursing can make or break a nurse. I thought I'd know what I was doing at the end of my nurse residency, or at least after one year of practice. Here is another painful fact: Competency doesn't magically appear at the end of the first year. The novice first-year nurse isn't transformed into a competent practitioner. Even now, there are some things I do very well and am genuinely proficient. Things like IV starts and interviewing patients are a piece of cake to me. But when new technologies or health system changes come into my practice, then, for a while, the novice stage begins again.

The nursing stories in this book are about some of my first-year nurse experiences in that nurse residency program. I hope you find that what I went through gives you a feel or basic grasp of what it's like to be a first-year registered nurse. Maybe after reading this, you just may think you could become a good nurse. You may well be correct.

In the words of Florence Nightingale, the woman widely considered to be the founder of modern nursing,

"The best nurses have the essential qualifications before they go to school."

Chapter One

"So never lose an opportunity of urging a practical beginning, however small, for it is wonderful how often in such matters the mustard-seed germinates and roots itself."
Florence Nightingale

Driving to my first day as an actual registered nurse on a real hospital unit, I was terrified. I hadn't slept well the night before. I had dreams of being late and coming into work dressed as a ballerina. You are such a twit, I thought. Think of the positive aspects of your situation. (Isn't that what everyone says who gives false reassurance to people who are afraid of the unknown?) Having no other coping ideas, I did it anyway. I told myself: You graduated from TSU, one of the top nursing schools, and passed the NCLEX exam with the minimal number of questions. You are going to be okay. You will be better than okay. Get it together, Kit!

The rising sun hit the Associates Only parking lot sign at just the right angle to partially blind me when I pulled in at 6:45 am. "Curse you Daylight Savings Time!" I muttered as I found something concrete to take the blame for my unease. "I come to work with sun in my eyes, and the sun doesn't set until after my bedtime. Can't state officials think of other things to do than play with the clock twice a year?" Feeling comfortably self-righteous and more in control, I eased my five-year-old Rallye Red Honda Civic into a great parking spot near the sidewalk.

I looked out at the three-story brick and stone building. Thompson Memorial Hospital, more commonly called TMH, was where I worked. My first day on a nursing unit as a registered nurse! This was the day I'd been planning for since high school.

The first thing I noticed was how quiet the hospital lobby was at 6:45 a.m. TMH is a medium-sized 245-bed hospital serving a suburban and rural population. It has been officially designated as a community hospital by the state. Only the security guard and a few early outpatient surgery patients had hospital business at this hour.

I was pleased to begin my professional nursing career in such a well-respected health care facility, without most of the severe patient care complexities that a nurse would encounter in the larger hospitals in the city. I was ready for this.

TMH hired me into the nurse residency program. The nurse residency program is designed to help new nursing graduates transition from student nurses to staff nurses. Every nurse I've ever talked to has told me that coming straight out of nursing school into a busy hospital environment is a jolting shock. The change from school to work often causes intense anxiety and even dismay for nurses in their first position after graduation. Rarely are new nurses prepared for the increase in responsibility and pace required of staff nurses.

I was aware that my direct patient involvement was limited in nursing school. Patient experiences were chosen by faculty so we student nurses could have a variety of patient encounters. Clinical time is short, usually 8-16 hours per week, and we cared for only one or two patients until the last semester. That meant my student experience was brief and not especially deep. I'm not sure how I could have done more clinicals, though. We balanced a schedule that was way more time-intensive in nursing school than my non-nursing student friends. Classes included nursing courses and others in liberal arts and the sciences. Each week, our class times and clinical experiences were about 20 hours. Including study time, nursing school semesters added up to 40-50 hour weekly commitment. That's a full-time job!

The short clinical experience in nursing school was probably the main reason the residency program was created. It takes time and careful attention to learn how to make safe nursing judgments and simultaneously respond to multiple demands. It's called nursing *practice* for a reason, you know. My residency program was six months long and scheduled to be completed by Christmas. I would spend the first three months on 3 North, one of the adult medical-surgical units. In months four and five, I would work with mentors on another nursing unit, the Intensive Care Unit. I was to return to 3 North for the last month. At that time, if my evaluations were satisfactory, I could apply for an open position within any unit at TMH. I don't know what would have happened if I was not successful. I didn't ask.

I loved the first week called "Onboarding," or beginning orientation for all new employees. TMH is part of a large multi-facility health organization called Trail State University Health System (TSUHS). The hospital's history, TSUHS's mission, and employee responsibilities were described so enthusiastically that I wanted to stand up and cheer! Managers and staff nurses from many nursing and support departments gave orientation presentations. Even though not all of the speakers were dazzling and some of the presentations honestly should be studied as promising treatments for insomnia, the Onboarding Department staff made sure there was little wasted time. The more mundane things like hours of work and breaks, grounds for discipline, the appeal of discipline, and taking time off with and without pay were covered in excruciating detail. There was some pay and health insurance paperwork to complete. I decided to take advantage of the hospital's 401K savings program. The payday schedule went directly into my calendar. (The first paycheck will come in two weeks!)

There was time for Basic Life Support for Health Professionals certification and some mandatory online education presentations. There was an online course test on the nurse's role in infection control, the health system's ethical framework of health care, disaster preparedness, and accurate care documentation in the EHR or electronic patient medical record. Our group completed a scavenger hunt as a tour of the hospital. I can now find the dietary department, the laboratories, radiology, and the surgical or operating room areas. I look startled in the picture taken for the hospital name badge granting me access to the medication cart, Medication Electronic Dispenser (MED), and to the EHR software, Thompson Integrated Medical Electronic System (TIMES). By the end of the week, I started to feel like I was becoming an essential part of the hospital staff. All these were just the first baby steps. Clinical experience takes up the remainder of the five months and three weeks. Working with patients is where reality confronts idealism in nurse residency. I was ready... I hoped...I prayed.

I met the nurse manager on the 3 North on Friday. The first three months of my nurse residency would be on 3 North. Emily Smith, the manager, assured me that the staff was eagerly waiting to welcome me. I knew that on Monday, the actual job would begin.

It seemed like everything was in sharp detail as I made my way from the lobby to 3 North that first morning. My new white nursing shoes squeaked on the gray and white terrazzo tile. There is a mural that spans the longest wall of the lobby commemorating the history of Thompson as a village founded by German farmers in the late 19th century to the dedication of TMH in 1955. The mural finishes with the 100th anniversary of the town's 1903 official founding. That morning I was so hyper-aware that the colors and characters of the mural seemed super clear and bright.

You could say I was feeling the energy of the hospital. You could also say I was overreacting to the situation. Just a little bit.

I needed to stop and take a second for a "time out." "Time outs" were strongly encouraged in nursing school and during orientation. They are a short period of time expressly set aside to give nurses a moment to be sure all is properly ready to begin a necessary procedure. I took a deep breath, let it out slowly and made sure I was ready. Name badge... check, stethoscope ... check, access codes to MED and TIMES... check and double-check.

The hospital gift shop window reminded me to stand tall and smooth my new scrubs. That morning, I carefully dressed in new navy blue scrubs, the color worn by RN's at TMH. I decided to swish my hair up into a ponytail to keep it controlled and neat. I even gave myself a manicure for this special occasion and topped my appropriate-length-not-too-long nails with a coat of Silk Pajamas soft pink nail polish.

I walked into the elevator and caught the eye of another nurse resident, Amanda Milton. We tried to look brave as we silently greeted each other. She lifted the fingers crossed sign, and I returned a thumbs up. I pushed the button for the third floor and fixed my gaze at the lights on the elevator control panel.

Maybe prayer wouldn't be a bad idea. Now I lay me down to sleep. Is that the best you can do? Oh God, please, help me do the right thing and not look as dim as I feel! Here you go, Kit Wilson, RN!

Chapter Two

"**Don't stop with your training. Aim higher. And--you will find if you are a true nurse, you have only just begun.**"
Florence Nightingale

Nodding goodbye to Amanda, I stepped out of the elevator and through the doors of 3 North. My first impression was one of cleanliness and calm. The walls were painted a soft green and framed prints of country scenes were hung on walls outside patient rooms. The air felt warmer than the lobby, and it had a mild yet not offensive odor. Three North is a 40-bed unit for generalized adult hospital care. It also serves as TMH's ICU step-down unit. In a blue smock with "Unit Clerk" embroidered on the pocket, a young woman sat behind the desk and looked up smiling as I slowly approached.

"Can I help you?" she asked.

"Yes. Is Mrs. Smith available?"

The unit clerk answered, "Emily? Yes, I think she is in her office down that hall, first door on your right."

"Thank you," I answered and headed toward the office.

As I approached the open door, Emily Smith rapidly walked out, pulling her knee-length white lab coat over street clothes. "Oh, good morning, Kit. Let me be the first to welcome you to 3 North officially. How are you? Ready for your first day?" Without giving me time to respond, Emily continued, "I'm off to a meeting, but I want you to meet your mentor, one of our most experienced nurses, Barb Mazer. She's expecting you. Oh Barb, Kit is here. Can I bring her over?

Emily waved and walked toward a middle-aged nurse whose appearance seemed to scream, "I'm experienced!" Also wearing navy scrubs, Barbara Mazer's name badge identified her as RN, BSN, Senior Staff Nurse. She seemed to be in her early 50s and had a slight smile on her face that I found instantly reassuring.

"Barb, this is Kit Wilson, the new nurse resident I told you about. She is all yours. I'm off." Emily turned to me and said, "Sorry I have to leave, but Barb will take good care of you." And with that, her wedge heels softly clicked down the hall, and she was gone.

"Hi Kit, it's nice to meet you. We're just about to start report; come on over," Barb said and led me into a nook of the nurse's station where five other nurses were sitting in a small circle. One voice was quietly giving information.

Barb spoke softly. "Here is a report sheet for you to take notes. Don't worry about getting everything down. We'll review taking and giving report later."

We sat down with the small group and took notes from the night shift nurses about 3 North patients' status. I had no idea which patients Barb had, but she took notes on every patient on a wing of 10 patients, so I did too. Remember, as a student nurse, I had only been responsible for report on two patients. My pen flew as I tried to listen and take down what I hoped was important night shift information. My brain was bouncing between, I have to get all this down, and I need to get the hell out of here. Thinking I could be a nurse was all a big mistake.

When report was over, Barb said to the group, "I want you all to meet Kit Wilson. She is going to be a new nurse resident on the floor, starting today."

Everyone acknowledged me, and one nurse said, "Good... new blood, we really need it. I hope she's going to nights."

"As you can tell, Susan, our night charge nurse, is very glad you're here," Barb said.

I tried to smile my most amiable smile. "It's nice to meet you all too. I'm sure I will learn a lot from you! By the way, you can call me Kit or Catherine. I answer to both."

"Well, nice to meet you Kit/Catherine! We can use the extra help; we are spread way too thin." Susan said. She seemed to be a few years older than me, probably in her late 20s or early 30s. Susan was petite, with a slightly crooked smile and wide crinkling eyes. She looked like she would be fun to get to know.

"I'm off, good night ... or maybe good morning; either way, have a good day!" and Susan left.

Barb stood up. "Let's check in on our patients; we have five today, with one transfer coming from ICU later this morning and at least two discharges. You will shadow me just for today, so you get a feeling of the floor layout and the patient population. Then we will work together as you increase your number of patients.

"First, let me describe the layout of 3 North so you'll be more familiar," Barb said. "Don't worry, there is no quiz on this, but it helps to have a general idea," she said and winked. "Also, each door has a sign on it, so no worries."

Barb described the medical surgical nursing unit's layout using a stick figure to illustrate. Three North has 40 beds. The unit is shaped like a Y with the center's nurses' station. The location of patient rooms, procedure rooms, nurses' conference/lunchroom, linen, and supply rooms were marked with initials.

Intent on learning the routine, I closely followed Barb out the nurses' station and down the hall, trying to imagine where I was on the stick figure diagram while also believing her words. No worries.

"We make every effort to keep the sickest patients as close to the nurses' station as possible. The number of patients assigned to an RN varies depending on the status of the patient and the shift. On average, an RN is assigned about 5 or 6 patients on the day shift and 7 or 8 on the night shift. We are lucky here on the day shift. Two RN's share a certified nurses' assistant or CNA to help us with basic patient care and errands. Night shift has one CNA for the entire unit. Tanya Smyth is our CNA today. Right now, she is doing a quick check-in to be sure no one needs immediate attention. Seeing the patients right after report is a good nursing practice. You can compare what you learned in report to how the person looks now, and you can check equipment, such as IVs and catheters, to be sure they are working properly. Our patients need to know who we are, so we will introduce ourselves, write our names as their nurse for today on the whiteboard in each room, and make sure there are no questions or unmet needs. You will want your patients to know and trust you."

Holy Toledo, do I have a lot to learn, I thought. Barb really knows what she's talking about. She sounds just like my instructors. I hoped I looked intelligent as I nodded and tried to keep good eye contact with Barb without staring like a deer in headlights. Which is how I felt.

We were greeted in room 310 by a female patient. She was out of bed and pacing the room in her robe and slippers. Her creased forehead, pursed mouth, crossed arms and, disheveled gray hair added up to a look of pronounced agitation.

"Good morning Mrs. Jones. How are you today? You seem upset."

Brenda Jones mumbled, "Humph! Don't care, just want to get out of here. Has my doctor been in yet? When is breakfast going to be served? Are you aware that it's late every morning? Doesn't matter anyhow. It will be cold and have no taste!" she grumbled.

Barb said, "Let me find out what's going on here. Did something happen this morning that has made you so upset?"

Brenda said, "I'm fine now. The tests were all negative, is that what you know too? I hope somebody found the time to tell you. Do you people talk to each other? I told them there was nothing wrong with me. I have things to do at home. My husband has to work extra hours and has made it crystal clear that he can't do everything. I can't lay around here forever!"

"Hospital routines can be frustrating sometimes," Barb said, "and home life does go on. Let's get things cleared up a bit for you. OK?" Brenda nodded and exhaled forcefully.

Barb went on, "Would you sit here on the side of the bed so I can get your vitals? I want to introduce you to Kit Wilson. Kit's an RN, and today is her first day with us. She will be tagging along with me to learn the ropes."

"Yeah, hi there," Brenda said as she sat on the side of the bed. Barb took her temperature, pulse, blood pressure, and oxygen saturation readings with the NIBP, the Noninvasive Blood Pressure monitor. The NIBP quickly measured Brenda's vital sign values, displaying them on the digital screen. "OK … blood pressure 140/88, pulse 86, O2 saturation at 98 and temperature 98.6." I watched her breathing and counted her respirations. "And respirations 14."

Barb asked a few pertinent questions centering around chest pain and ease of breathing. She listened to Brenda's lung and heart sounds and lightly touched her ankles. "No pain, no dyspnea, no dependent edema," she said softly to herself and wrote the values on her note sheet.

She looked up at Brenda. "Dyspnea is difficulty breathing and, by touching your ankles, I can assess if your ankles are swollen from fluid retention," she said. "Your findings are right in line with what we heard from the night shift and what you think too. Let me go out and see if I can get an answer to your questions. I'll be back shortly. Here's your call light if you need anything before I return." Barb put our names on the whiteboard and left the room.

I continued to follow Barb dutifully. She never stopped talking to me. "Brenda Jones had severe chest pain yesterday morning and was admitted for testing. She was ordered a stress test, EKG, an echocardiogram to assess her heart muscle and valves, lab studies and observation. All results were within normal limits. There were no findings of heart disease. She wants out and I don't blame her. What did you notice about her and, what did you think about her exam?"

With the flood of information I had just received, I said the only two things I could think of: Brenda's blood pressure was higher than recommended, and her pacing around the room and passive-aggressive remarks indicated some concerns about coping with being in the hospital.

"Good," said Barb. "Good observations. Brenda agrees that her lifestyle needs some changes. She will readily admit that she doesn't have the control she wants in her life. Although it didn't seem so this morning, Brenda's aware that her symptoms were made worse by a stressful event. She was recently laid off because she was caring for her ill mother. Her mother died less than two months ago. You remember from nursing school that bringing your physical body to healthy levels takes commitment and support. Coping with stress is not as easy as it sounds. Let's talk to her cardiologist when she makes rounds and ask for a referral to the clinical nurse specialist. The CNS can work with Brenda and her family to help work out a plan to manage the recent losses and changes in her life. We're lucky to have this advanced practice nurse to help patients like Brenda before she has further health problems."

"Oh yes," I said, nodding thoughtfully, hoping I didn't look like a bobblehead.

We made our way down the hall to room 312. There was a guy in his mid-thirties with dark hair in the bed, watching TV. "Good morning, Bill. How are you feeling today?" asked Barb.

"Not too bad, Barb, the pain is a little less than yesterday. Who's this?" he said, looking at me.

"This is Kit Wilson, she's a new nurse here on the floor, and it is her first day."

"Hi, Kit. Nice to meet you," Bill said and rather formally offered a handshake.

"Bill had his toxic appendix out late yesterday afternoon. He is on antibiotics, drinking clear liquids, and doing very well post-operatively. His last pain medication was at midnight, and he was up walking a little last evening. We're here to do our first check, Bill. Kit, would you like to do the honors and get Bill's vitals? I see Tanya has filled your water pitcher."

"Of course!" I put the blood pressure cuff around the patient's arm and started the BP monitor automatic cycle. After putting a clean cover on the probe, I put the thermometer in his mouth. I remembered that since Bill's appendix ruptured before surgery yesterday, he was at a high risk for abdominal infection, which can be life-threatening. "OK, 125/78 and 89.6 temp."

"Wow. I didn't realize I was that cold," Bill responded, laughing immediately.

"Ohh, I mean 98.6." How stupid of me; I can't believe I did that. I have taken a million temperatures. Take a deep breath and get a grip!

"That's OK, Kit, don't worry about it ... a simple mistake," Barb said. "It's common to have a triple dose of anxiety on the first day."

She turned to the patient. "Your incision site looks good under the invisible dressing, Bill. No swelling, drainage, or redness. Let's see how your lab tests come back this morning and, hopefully, talk your surgeon into springing you out of this place," Barb said with a smile and walked out the room. I hurried right behind her down the hall to the next room.

The double room on this wing was 314. On this day, only one person was in the room. The bed nearest the door was saved for a transfer patient from the Intensive Care Unit later in the morning. The sole occupant had his eyes closed.

"Mr. Koncel, how are you feeling?" Barb asked.

"Lousy. Isn't that how I am supposed to feel in a hospital? Truthfully? I'm just pooped out," he said. The color of his face was an intense red, and his speech was slow. Mr. Koncel was a Type I diabetic dependent on insulin to keep his blood sugar in an acceptable range. He had been admitted for overnight observation after a low blood sugar episode resulted in an EMT visit to his home.

"Kit, would you please get his vitals? I want to listen to his heart and lungs," Barb asked.

"Right away." I could hear the urgency in her voice and got the vital signs monitored quickly. His blood pressure was 170/94, his pulse was 58 and slightly irregular, and his respirations were 18. I saw from my report notes that his 6:00 am blood sugar was 110, which was acceptable.

"That blood pressure is pretty high for you compared with what you had yesterday and last night."

Barb repeated the BP to verify my reading. The result was similar. During careful questioning about chest pain, difficulty breathing, abdominal tenderness, and a pulse check in his wrists and feet, Barb learned that Mr. Koncel was "tired as hell." He had no other negative symptoms. She said, "I'll let your doctor know this and see what he wants to do."

Barb walked toward the nurses' station just a bit faster this time. "I don't like Mr. Koncel's assessment findings this morning. His blood pressure doesn't usually run that high; his slow and irregular heart rate and fatigue are not typical. Something is going on," Barb said. As an experienced RN, Barb had the experience to analyze his assessment and recognize that his condition was deteriorating. I was frantically thinking about putting together all the data from Mr. Koncel's assessment in a seemingly-intelligent way.

As we walked into the station, Barb said to the unit clerk, "Mary, will you page Dr. Biels or his Nurse Practitioner for me right away and give me a yell when there is a response?"

"Of course," Mary picked up the phone.

Chapter Three

"There is a time for all things—A time to be trained and a time to use our training."
Florence Nightingale

B arb grabbed a telemetry transmitter, five EKG patches from the drawer, and a pulse oximeter probe. She continued to teach me by reviewing the combined assessment findings of flushed coloring, extreme tiredness, and higher systolic and diastolic blood pressure than was usual for this middle-aged man. "His heart rate is in the lower normal limit of normal, and it will be important to be sure there aren't cardiac rhythm problems. We want to be sure that he's oxygenating well, so we will check his pulse oximetry." I nodded and remembered that the pulse ox or O2 Sat measures the percentage of oxygen in red blood cells and should be between 96-100 percent.

"Let's not forget that we'll give Mr. Koncel an explanation about why we're doing what we are doing and allow him to voice any questions or worries. It will be important for us to behave calmly and in a matter-of-fact way. It's not an emergency at this point, and we certainly don't want him to think we're overly concerned."

That's easy for you to say, I thought. I've only put on telemetry patches three times in a skill lab. I'm glad Barb knows what to do.

Barb was back in the room with a calm smile. "Mr. Koncel, I'm going to take your blood pressure once more. You're getting the three-times-for-the-price-of-one blood pressure special today," she gently joked. "Then, because you're so tired and your blood pressure is up a bit, I want to get you connected to a heart monitor. The nurses will be able to see your heart rhythm on the monitor at the nurses' station and here in the room."

Barb put the five round EKG patches on his chest and connected the patches to the clips from the telemetry transmitter. She took the bedside monitor out of Standby mode and selected his transmitter number. His EKG rhythm started marching across the screen as a regular and slow normal sinus rhythm at 60 beats per minute. Then, an extra wide beat popped up on the monitor, followed by the slow normal sinus rhythm. Barb told Mr. Koncel that his primary heart rhythm was called slow sinus rhythm or bradycardia. "Every so often, you have an extra beat that is called a PVC or premature ventricular contraction. The padded clip on your finger measures the amount of oxygen in your blood."

"Kit, let's get Mr. Koncel some O2 at two liters per minute (LPM)."

I set up the oxygen, placed a cannula in Mr. Koncel's nose, and set the oxygen flow.

Barb paused after we had finished. She waited a moment to assess how well he was coping with all the new information and equipment. "Do you have any questions about what I've said? I've paged Dr. Biel, and I want to see what we can do to help you feel better." Mr. Koncel nodded and closed his eyes.

Barb led me to the side of the nurses' station where the central monitor bank was located. All the patients who had cardiac and pulse ox monitors had displays here. "See here," Barb pointed to Mr. Koncel's display, "he periodically has PVCs. Remember, his pulse oximetry reading was 93. Tell me what that could indicate."

I was ready with the answer. "Mr. Koncel's heart is irritable, and his ventricles are firing some PVCs that are not effective because they don't perfuse oxygen to his vital organs. That can be dangerous if allowed to continue and could lead to a lethal cardiac rhythm," I took a deep breath. "His pulse oximetry is supposed to be 96 to 100 normally. His reading of 93 shows he's doesn't have enough oxygen in his system."

Barb nodded, smiled and I nearly fainted with relief. Wow, where did that come from? I have no idea what made me so accurately glib to this day. I guess I did know a little something.

"Barb, I have Dr. Biels on the phone," said Mary.

"Good!" Barb reached for the phone. "Dr. Biels, this is Barb Mazer, I am taking care of Jack Koncel, and I'm concerned. His BP is running 170-180/90-94. I've placed him on a monitor. His rhythm is sinus brady at 60 with occasional PVC's. His pulse ox is 93. We have O2 on at 2 LPM by cannula. He's reporting extreme fatigue but is alert and has no other signs." Barb listened on the phone and finally answered, "Good ...yes ... OK, I will do that."

Barb hung up. "Let's check to be sure his IV is functioning well because we will be giving some medications to decrease the heart's irritability. The doctor is at Grand Rounds reviewing past cases. He's on his way up to see him."

The Central Monitor Station alarm blunted her last few words. It was a yellow alert alarm indicating Mr. Koncel had more PVCs.

Barb directed me, "Just to be safe, let's get a crash cart outside his room."

I began to get worried. Barb's voice had a new note of concern. Mr. Koncel's problems were ramping up quickly. Accurate and swift nursing judgment was needed, and I was deeply grateful that Barb was in charge of that and not me.

I walked to the crash cart and unplugged the defibrillator on top. The central station alarm rang again. In an ordinary yet slightly elevated voice, the unit clerk said, "Red alarm. Room 314."

I remembered from hospital orientation that a red flashing light over a patient's cardiac monitor meant detection of a dangerous heart rhythm.

"Damn," said Barb softly, looking at the monitor. "Ventricular tachycardia." She walked swiftly into the room, and I followed, lugging the crash cart.

"Mr. Koncel, are you OK? Barb asked. She stood by his bed and felt the carotid pulse on his neck, and looked at the monitor, continuing to call his name.

Mr. Koncel was pale and sweating and not responding. Then, his eyes rolled back in his head.

Barb called Mary on the room's intercom, saying in a regular voice, "Mary, call a code, please. Kit, get that crash cart in the room."

I brought the cart next to the bed and broke the plastic lock on the drug drawers so that they could be accessed easily. I had seen two codes before in school and had a basic idea what was going to happen.

The hospital intercom blared the same message three times:

"ATTENTION THOMPSON MEMORIAL HOSPITAL, CODE BLUE ROOM 314

"ATTENTION THOMPSON MEMORIAL HOSPITAL, CODE BLUE ROOM 314

"ATTENTION THOMPSON MEMORIAL HOSPITAL, CODE BLUE ROOM 314"

Suddenly, many other nurses and staff quickly walked in. I knew they were from the "Code Team" that had spoken to us during hospital orientation. Their job was to coordinate and assist with treating life-threatening situations. Mr. Koncel's cardiac rhythm certainly fell in that category.

I moved the first bed out of the room at the brisk request of the respiratory therapist who had taken position at Mr. Koncel's head. The bed was now completely flat and raised to its highest position. One of the team members watched the cardiac monitor in the room, calling out the heart rhythm. The members called out their actions beginning with cardiopulmonary resuscitation. "Starting CPR!"

Barb moved around the crowd of professionals and tapped me on the shoulder. "Come here, Kit. This is a great learning experience for you. Just stay out of the way." I didn't need to be told twice. I moved back and watched with rapt attention. This was so cool. This was so outside my comfort zone!

Someone had taken the backboard from the crash cart and put it under Mr. Koncel's back. CPR had started. A member of the Code Team was giving chest compressions while the respiratory therapist was using a bag and mask connected to wall oxygen to assist Mr. Koncel's breathing.

A man with a suit and tie walked in. This must be Dr. Biels, I correctly assumed.

I was getting into the tempo and noticed something that Barb should know. "Shouldn't they give atropine now?" I asked. "That's what we learned in school for a slow heart rate. He had bradycardia, remember?"

Barb stared at me for a second and blinked. "Not in this case. We can talk about this later when we can discuss everything."

The heart rhythm on the display didn't look like a proper rhythm at all. It looked like tiny squiggles on the screen. This is exactly what ventricular fibrillation looks like: uncoordinated and ineffective contractions within the heart's ventricles. If not treated, it will be fatal for the patient.

Dr. Biels very calmly and clearly followed the American Heart Association protocol for full cardiac arrest. Medications, CPR, and defibrillation were given in a precise order and within a specific time frame, followed by repeat assessments of the patient's response. Mr. Koncel required defibrillation. A high-pitched whistle came from the defibrillator as it charged. One of the nurses put pads on Mr. Koncel's chest, and another pushed the paddles tight against his chest.

"CLEAR!" said the person with the paddles. Everyone stepped back from the patient and the bed to avoid contact with the shock from the defibrillator. The defibrillator fired a high voltage into Mr. Koncel, making his chest lift off the bed.

"OK, now what do we have? asked Dr. Biels as he reassessed Mr. Koncel's status. All eyes went to the monitor on the defibrillator. It was a flat line. "Continue CPR."

The person giving chest compressions started up again, and the therapist continued to push oxygen into his lungs. CPR continued for another two minutes.

Barb watched the clock and made notes because documenting the times of all medications and treatments must be carefully recorded during a code.

Dr. Biels said, "OK, stop and let's see what's going on." They paused CPR, and all eyes focused on the monitor again. Mr. Koncel had a normal sinus rhythm, at a rate of 65, and no further PVCs for now.

"Great work, everyone! Let's get a drip going in that IV to calm down the myocardium. Thank you, I am sure that Jack appreciates your excellent efforts."

Barb softly said, "Notice how his rhythm is stabilizing." She continued to point out the rationale for medications and treatments Mr. Koncel had received. He was breathing on his own with an oxygen mask and inflating bag over his nose and mouth.

Emily Smith was also in the room watching what was going on. Emily had stayed on the side of the room and seemed pleased to see the Code Team and 3 North staff working so well together. I overheard Emily tell Dr. Biels that an Intensive Care Unit (ICU) bed was ready for Mr. Koncel.

As the Code Team left the room, we cleaned up the room and Mr. Koncel. Most of the packaging from the disposables had been dropped on the floor. Mr. Koncel's bed was a mess.

Barb was amazing. She never stopped telling me about what had happened during the Code and who had responded to the Code. She frequently assessed Mr. Koncel and his monitor readings. She also explained why atropine was an inadequate medication to respond to a life-threatening heart rhythm such as ventricular tachycardia or ventricular fibrillation. As we finished getting the bed straightened, Mr. Koncel started to wake up.

"What happened... my chest hurts," he asked, grimacing.

Barb gave him a brief explanation of what had happened. She reassured him that he was stable now and could rest while we worked. Someone would be in soon with some pain medication for him. She told him that he would be transferred to ICU so the nurses could more closely monitor him.

After the ICU team arrived to transfer Mr. Koncel, we walked to the break room and took a deep breath. It seemed hours instead of 28 minutes since the Code Blue began. It wasn't even 8:30 am! I was ready for some coffee and a donut. Barb, however, was ready for us to finish our initial rounds of the rest of their patients. The CNA and two other nurses from the unit quickly updated and assured Barb that no patient was ignored despite the emergency.

Barb sighed, "It's teamwork that keeps me working on 3 North. Don't ever fall into the trap of focusing only on 'your' patients that you are assigned on a given day. It takes practice but start today to be aware of what is going on in the rest of the unit. Helping your colleagues with all their other patients' immediate direct nursing needs will allow them to focus on the critical issues in front of them."

There was one more big surprise that first day. Lunch was a 15-minute affair taken in the break room. Thankfully, vending machines were available outside 3 North since I hadn't thought to pack a lunch or snack.

"It's one of the axioms in hospital staff nursing," Barb told her. "Taking a lunch break in the cafeteria is rare. Because of the speed with which patients are treated and discharged from the hospital, and the acuity level of patients each RN is assigned, a quick, short lunch break is taken when you can."

She smiled, "Not to be too personal here, kiddo but get to the bathroom too whenever you have the chance. Some days that's an easy thing to forget and can get you into infection trouble. Or at least make you wonder why your stomach hurts at the end of your shift."

This news about the lunch break caught me off guard. My mind was working overtime to keep the patient information straight. When we were in school, nurses at University Hospital told us that nurses in community hospitals didn't work as hard as those in the big hospitals. We had a 45 minutes break each day for lunch during the Onboarding Week. I knew I wouldn't get that long for lunch every day but, for sure, 30 minutes. And in the cafeteria where they had real food. Another nursing myth was out the window only six hours into my first shift.

At 7:00 pm, I listened carefully as Barb gave report. The amount of detail she passed on to the night shift about the day shift was awe-inspiring. Just the fact that I was present for all of it was unbelievable!

Barb walked me to my car. "You'll catch on, kiddo. You had a pretty decent first day, and we will work together for the next month. Have a relaxing night!"

It was still daylight at 7:45 pm. I put on my sunglasses, doubly happy for grabbing such a close parking spot 13 hours earlier. I had survived my first day as a registered nurse. Daylight Savings Time suddenly didn't seem such a big deal.

Chapter Four

"Live life when you have it. Life is a splendid
gift-there is nothing small about it."
Florence Nightingale

The first few months as a working RN, I lived with my parents and slept in my childhood room. It was a fine enough arrangement, but I had bigger plans. As soon as I saved a little, I was determined to get my own place. It seemed like the next logical step on my way to becoming a fully functioning adult. I had my eye on a possible apartment complex in our town. But first things first. My priority was making enough money to save for a security deposit.

My mom and dad were thrilled to have me "at home" again. I hadn't spent more than a couple of weeks at a time there since I started in the nursing program two years ago. My younger brothers were less thrilled because they had to share the "kids' bathroom" again with one more kid. I could not believe how much time my baby brothers spent primping and preening in the bathroom. To be fair, mom and dad only charged me a little bit of rent so that I could save for an apartment, and the boys almost never used my good shampoo and body wash.

The biggest problem with being home was that we were all up in each other's business. To be specific, they were all up in my business. Not just idle curiosity, but incredibly nosey. Questions like: What's it like as a nurse? Did you see anything

gross today? Why are you reading that book? I have a better one
for you. Did you meet any cute guys at the hospital?

I'm an introvert by nature. I was used to having some privacy at school. My suite mates didn't ask for details about my
day when I came in, and for sure, they never commented on
the poor nutritional choices I made in candy bars or the literary
value of the fiction I read. I got used to doing things to relax,
like reading what I liked and streaming Grey's Anatomy and
chatting with friends down the hall or watching away games at
The Library, which was the ironic name of the best bar on cam-
pus. I could be more sociable for sure, but the interaction that
my family expected from me was draining my energy on top of
my nurse residency.

Telling you about my immediate family can help explain
why I can feel both so lucky and yet annoyed to have all of them
in my life. Knowing a little about them might help explain how I
got through the shock of my first paycheck. I don't mean to give
you more information than you need or want to know. You can
skip ahead if you wish to, but I'll bet you can relate to some of it.

There are six of us living in Thompson. I'm the only girl
kid, and everybody has a nickname. Here are our family values:

Work hard to succeed at what you choose to do,

Give cheerfully to others who need help,

Don't think you're a bigger deal than other people because
you're not,

Never use the F word in Mom's presence. OK, I made up
#4, but that makes it no less true.

My mom is Victoria Wilson. She goes by Vicki and is an
elementary school teacher. Mom has taught 4th grade for as long
as I can remember. She celebrates small family events with her
famous "dinner parties." Unless you are out of town or bleeding by the roadside, you are expected to be there. Mom's dinner
parties are just Sunday suppers that have a theme. Mom decides
the theme, and we all go along with it. She is nothing if not

imaginative. Last Sunday, we celebrated my first paycheck with sesame peanut grilled chicken, green beans, freshly made bread, and ice water. Dessert was peanut butter and chocolate cookies. Get it? Making peanuts? Bread and water? Being on a budget? So eye rollingly clever!

My dad is Andrew Wilson. Dad is the reason we all have nicknames. He thinks nicknames show love. Again, like mom's themed dinners, we go along with Dad's nickname quirk. Dad is a pharmacist. He's the manager of Thompson Pharmacy and Wellness. From cashiers to shelf stockers to the other pharmacists and technicians, everyone at the store reports to Dad. He has taken care of the medication needs for people in town for so long that some will call Pharmacist Andy for an opinion before calling their doctor. He is my role model for a professional health care team player. Dad is the least flappable person I know and calmed me down plenty of times in nursing school when I was sure I would fail on a paper or care plan or presentation. Mom calls him the Kit Whisperer.

I have three brothers. Edward or Teddy is the oldest. He lives in a small house he just purchased and teaches math at Thompson High School. Teddy is four years older than I am. Teddy takes his job as a teacher seriously. Since he is a very mature adult (in his own eyes, that is), he tries to tell me what to do. We sort of get along when he's not trying to be my third parent. When I moved home, he devoted his energy to putting me on a budget. I'm sure he carried a budget spreadsheet titled Kit's Financial Life in his back pocket.

Matthew is 13 months younger than I am. Matt and I are jokingly referred to as Irish Twins because we are so close in age. His nickname is Maddy, but you should not ever call him that unless you are in our family. Since high school, he has wanted to be called Matt. My parents, brothers, and I pay no attention to Maddy's name preference. He is a lot of fun and was so good at making friends at TSU that he had a hard time remembering that he was there to go to school. Right now, he's taking time off from college and working at the Thompson Lumber Company. He is also back in his childhood room. Maddy and I have been protective of each other since he came home from the hospital.

Our youngest brother is Kyle. Yes, he has a nickname too. It's Kai. He describes himself as almost 16 and almost a junior in high school. He's what mom and dad tell as "the best surprise they ever had." Kai is sweet and still thinks I'm lovely, so I love him best of all. Teddy and Kai pretend they don't know each other while at school so that no one will think there is any favoritism. I'm not sure, but I'd bet they didn't fool anyone.

Except for Gram, Jennifer (Jen) Wilson, that's my family. I'll save tales about Gram for now. Gram is Dad's mother and lives in San Davers, not too far from TSU. She is a nurse and still works full-time. She is an essential part of my life, so she gets a separate piece of the story.

But, now for the rest of the First Paycheck saga.

Chapter Five

"(My records) would show subscribers how their money was being spent, what amount of good was really being done with it, or whether the money was not doing mischief rather than good."

Florence Nightingale

On the third Friday as an RN at Thompson Hospital, I got my first paycheck. Well, not an actual check, but money deposited in my bank account. I can check my TMH employee account online to check earnings, deductions, and deposits.

I want to be clear that it's not that I'd never worked before or had a paycheck. I knew that taxes and other things were taken out of gross income. I worked at the State Health Department Clinic for the last two summers of college. My job was part of a college scholarship program where I got some tuition paid, made precisely minimum wage, and there were no papers or presentations to prepare. It was a fine summer job. Cheap student housing included donuts, juice, and coffee in the mornings. In those gloriously simple times, I was only concerned with making enough money to buy gas, smoothies, music, car insurance, downloads, and other college essentials.

My first real paycheck as an RN was supposed to be Big. The hospital was paying me almost three times what I made at the health department. I had it all calculated. There was a base salary, and then I got a $5000 sign-on bonus spread out over 12 months for being an RN with a BSN. Then, the differentials.

Differentials are so cool. They are extra money paid every hour the nurse works undesirable hours. Undesirable hours are nights and weekends. That means every weekend I worked, I got $3.00 extra per hour, and when I worked the night shift, there was another $2.50 per hour. As you can see, I was going to be rolling in dough.

It didn't exactly work out that way. My first paycheck was like a poke in the eye. I needed help to figure out how to get out of my parents' house and be on my own. At the rate TMH was handing out money, I'd be looking at a pink bedspread until I was 30. As much as I loathed to admit it, this was a job for Teddy.

On Sunday, I met Teddy at the front door and started talking before the door closed behind him. "OK, I need your help. Bring out the advice. I just got my paycheck, and it seems that what I bring home every two weeks is almost half what the apartment of my dreams costs every month."

"Oh yes," he said, grinning like one of the Sunday morning financial tricksters on cable. "I've worked out a system where you can save money and get what you want. It's as easy as 60-30-10. It's fun."

"Yeah, whatever," I said. "As long as it doesn't involve spreadsheets and I can get my own place before I'm 30."

Teddy means well, and he can be excused for acting like Mr. Big Bucks. He's only 26 and owns a house, and his car isn't falling apart. Teddy's a teacher, and if you haven't been paying attention, they don't make a lot of money. He works in the summer tutoring overachieving kids in ACT math and working for his buddy's moving company, *2 Buffs and a Truck*. I don't care what you say; my big brother knows how to squeeze money.

Kit's First Paycheck was the topic du jour as the entire family weighed in on my business at Sunday supper. Over the "making peanuts" theme, everybody, except Kai, shared their first paycheck stories. It turns out that the number of deductions taken out of their first paycheck was a shock for almost everybody. Federal tax, State tax, City tax, health insurance, dental insurance, eye insurance, Old Age/Social Security, School tax, Some-Initials-That-I-Didn't-Understand tax, and 401K retirement. Teddy assured me I would be happy when my next pairs of contacts were "free" and that I was going to retire in the relative lap of luxury because of my 401K saving plan. I was still unable to work up a lot of gratitude for an event that was about 45 years in the future.

After dinner, the other boys helped with the dishes so that Teddy and I could figure out how I could get myself into the new apartment complex on Centenary Road. It has an inside/outside pool and fitness center, garage parking, and a one-bedroom layout that is perfect for me. It's called Chateau Bordeaux! What a great name. Trust me, that's super sophisticated for Thompson.

The long and short of Teddy's 60-30-10 plan is to spend 60 percent of your take-home pay on Necessities and 30 percent on Extras or Want to Have Things, and 10 percent on Personal Savings. I was already saving in a 401 K for retirement, so I was confident that I was ahead of the game. At first, I loved Teddy's little formula. My dream apartment costs exactly 60 percent of my take-home salary each month. So, I figured all I had to do was save for the security deposit, and I was in business. Based on my calculations, I was spending my money for good, not for mischief or unneeded purchases.

However, the Necessities category was out to torment me. It also included food, utilities, insurance co-pays, gas, and car insurance. That knocked my affordability quotient down from a one-bedroom into the studio (one room for living and sleeping with a bathroom and walk-in closet) apartment category at the Chateau Bordeaux. Teddy suggested I look for a less expensive option for my first apartment. Hmm. We'll see. Perhaps I was living in LaLa Land, but I wasn't going to give up so easily.

We played with the numbers, and when I put another 10 percent in Necessities and used 25 percent for Extras like new clothes, meals out, and credit cards and 5 percent to save, I was still $268.00 short of my dream apartment every month.

The coup de grace was when Teddy asked me how I planned to furnish the apartment. How do I know? Ask mom and dad? Take my pink twin bed set from my room at home? Throw me a New Apartment shower?

Even though I was still technically not Chateau Bordeaux ready, I felt better after getting the numbers down on paper. Now I had a plan, even if I was looking at staying with my parents for at least three more months and maybe more if my Furnish Kit's Apartment shower idea didn't take off.

That night I dreamed of sofa beds and bath towels and shower curtains and Kitchen In A Box from Amazon.

Chapter Six

"**I think one's feelings waste themselves in words; they ought all to be distilled into actions which bring results.**"
Florence Nightingale

The first month of residency orientation went by quickly. It's astonishing how much I learned. I began to feel more settled when I walked into the hospital and smelled the ultrafiltered air. The briskness of the ventilation almost had a clear hue. I could time the elevator almost to the moment the bell pinged. Many hospital staff climbed the stairs from Main to their floor. So, to round out my residency experiences, I did too. A couple of times. There are six sets of stairs from Main to Three. I decided to save my energy for the unit and usually took the elevator.

The 3 North routines began to take on a logical feel. Within two weeks, I felt less panicked when making patient rounds. Well, panicked might be too strong a word. It's probably more accurate to say I didn't feel a wave of anxiety every time I walked into a new patient's room. Believe me, that was progress. Assessment became more natural. I began to translate the feel of skin hydration and intact status into concise words. Barb would periodically reassess one of my patients. More and more often, her findings of heart and lung sounds were the same as mine. I was able to insert IVs with more accuracy. The plastic IV needle sheath began to feel more comfortable, as did the smooth insertion of the catheter and removal of the needle after blood return. One day, after having about ten successful insertions, I noticed my gloved hands had stopped trembling. My documentation in the TIMES medical record even earned Barb's praise twice. So, residency was all hunky-dory, right? Hardly. The fact was I never seemed to catch up. From the moment I received report from the night shift until I was giving report to the night shift 12 hours later, I was always behind. My time with patients was too short. I couldn't spend any meaningful moments talking therapeutically with patients and still get all my work done.

Barb continued to be my mentor, and every day she gave me more to do. Honestly, she never lost patience with me and was a good advisor. Yet, some of Barb's actions were frankly mysterious. Her ability to know what I was doing well and what I needed to do over or learn differently was almost scary. Like eyes in the back of her head scary. At any rate, she never let up, and she never left me all alone. On the other hand, I never once felt that I had it all together.

Barb thought my frustration with not having time to talk to my patients could be helped if I worked more on what she called "focused communication." That started to be a problem for me. I wanted to let patients know me and trust me. I wanted my patients to confidently tell me their feelings so I could show them my compassion and empathy. Barb thought I would show compassion better if I promptly met their nursing needs, answered their questions, taught them skills they would need at home, and regularly documented care throughout the day. Obviously, I thought, she was an old nurse stuck in just doing her duty for patients.

Barb always complimented one or two things I did every day, but I never felt as though she thought I was doing a great job. I was a good student nurse, and I expected to be a good RN. I deserved more positive reinforcement. I was starting to feel resentful.

After careful musing, I came to believe that sometimes Barb had unrealistic expectations. She was patient most of the time, but after the first week, she became more demanding. I had expected to have a mentor who allowed me to increase my speed at my own pace. I needed a more individualized nurse residency.

After all, I reasoned, I'm a visual and hands-on learner. I need to take things slowly and practice a few times before moving on to the next task. Barb probably wasn't familiar with the current thinking about learning styles. She was probably like the old-fashioned nurses we learned about in school that are only focused on tasks and not the patient as a person. She just didn't realize how she made me feel sometimes and how her thoughts about communication would make me compromise what I'd learned in school about nurse-patient relationships. That was not right. I decided to sort of ease into the subject when we met.

Barb and I made it a practice to sit down at the end of every shift for a 10-minute debriefing of the day's events. At the end of the fifth day shift, I knew it was best to tell Barb that she made me feel inadequate at times and that her approach was not conducive to positive orientation.

Barb sighed. "Learning how to become a functioning RN may be one of the hardest things you'll ever do, kiddo. You'll never learn to practice at an optimal level if I tell you that you're doing OK at everything. You're coming along, Kit, but your assessment skills and organization need to pick up."

I was so earnest. "I can't pick up quickly if my mind isn't programmed to move that fast. I need more time and more patience while I'm learning. In school, we were told that nursing is different today. We don't just perform tasks. We think conceptually about our patients. We care deeply about our patients and our learning styles help us know how to do that best."

Barb nodded. "That is certainly true. Many things have changed in the 30 years since I was a new graduate. But since I've been in practice, we nurses have been expected to analyze many parts of a situation and practice holistic nursing care.

However, the whole person concept of nursing is not new to nursing, Kit. We show respect and compassion in the way we organize the care we deliver as well as in our communication with patients and families."

Does Barb even understand up-to-date nursing? I wondered.

"I know about holism," I said somewhat defensively.

"You know what I think?" Barb asked. "It's easier to know some of this nursing stuff than to understand it and put it into practice."

"Yes!" Finally, she understood what I was saying. "That's what I meant."

Barb's countenance softened. "I know you learned in school that it was acceptable to use a learning preference to explain how fast you pick up on new things. I understand and respect whatever your learning style might be, but I have to tell you what others may not tell you. They will talk behind your back. Colleagues won't tell you if you're too slow or lack critical thinking skills."

I sat back, furious at the tears that gathered in my eyes. This conversation wasn't going the way it was supposed to go. "OK. Thanks for being honest. Maybe I could help the other nurses by explaining what it's like to be a visual learner."

"Let's concentrate on just you right now. I know you're smart enough to do this. Perhaps you could use your understanding of your personal learning style to help with your organization and time management. I'm sure some techniques would be helpful to a visual learner. I'm not criticizing and would tell you if there was any serious concern with your progress," Barb paused and leaned forward. "This may be hard to hear, but speaking of habits you will want to change, try to get here earlier than 6:55 a.m. The shift report starts at 7:00 a.m. We don't enjoy waiting for you to put away your things, greet everyone, and get settled to start report. Let's put an end to your unit nickname Just-in-Time-Kit. I can almost guarantee you that getting here at least

15 minutes before report will help you organize and prioritize a whole lot better."

"Just-in-Time-Kit! That's terrible! How humiliating. I'll never be able to look at the other nurses in the eyes again." I nearly jumped up in anger.

"Kit, I tell you these things because you can't see them yourself. I've got your back. I want you to succeed as an RN. The real-life nursing culture is different in some important ways from nursing school. We all work in close surroundings, and we need to depend on each other. Nicknames can be embarrassing. If we pay attention, they can help too."

Barb paused to let me absorb my work's less than stellar evaluation. As an experienced mentor, she knew that new graduates didn't take criticism well, even kindly delivered. A nurse's first job is intense and especially important. How other nurses treat new graduates can be a significant factor in determining whether they stay in nursing or leave.

Barb seemed to consider her following words carefully. "There is usually one of a couple of reactions new nurses have to coaching from a mentor. The first is self-righteous indignation. You might think, 'No one ever told me that when I was in school. These nurses don't understand. They have no right to be critical! This makes me furious.' Another reaction is to feel dumb and maybe a little mortified. You might think, 'I'm so stupid. I'll never get this stuff. It's too much for me. I might as well quit now.' I get it, Kit. But truthfully, neither one of these reactions is what is intended with this nickname. That's why your colleagues asked me to tell you about your just-in-time-ness. In this part of your nurse residency program, I'm the person who will usually coach you about good performance and areas that need, shall we say, some strengthening. You know that the nurse residency program is not awfully long. You will be expected to carry a full load when you finish, and no one will cut you any slack. I'll help you hear the hard things in private. Please take it as another piece of information that wasn't specifically covered in nursing school. Just think about it. OK, kiddo?"

I nodded and let Barb give me a quick hug. But the doubts cropped up. Is nursing for me? Hospital nursing in real life isn't what I thought it would be. It seems I was spending a whole lot of time trying to catch up with patients' needs, physician demands, communication with other departments, and documenting every little thing. There was not much space at all to find satisfaction in helping people. Nursing seemed to be one big race to the 12-hour finish line. Nurses who got it all done were the winners. Here's the worst part. I was even starting to resent the patients' demands on me. I hated those thoughts. But really, how do other nurses do it? Patients would write letters about how compassionate some of the nurses were. These usually were the nurses who seemed to finish their work calmly. I didn't get it. What am I missing? How can I let my patients know how empathic I am if I'm always running around? How can running around and getting the never-ending stuff done make patients love the nurse? This is an insane job.

Chapter Seven

How very little can be done under the spirit of fear.
                                    Florence Nightingale

I sometimes wondered whether I was cut out to be a nurse in those first weeks. But Amanda Milton was the tipping point. The first couple days of residency, I usually walked into the hospital from the parking lot with Amanda, my friend from hospital orientation. She and I shared an elevator that first morning. Amanda's residency started on 3 South, the other adult medical-surgical unit at TMH. We were supposed to be together for ICU orientation beginning the third month. Amanda is a tall young woman with flawless pale skin, brown eyes, and a French braid wrapped around her head. She has a regal bearing and a confident smile. The first week, we admitted that nursing was different from what we thought, but we both were excited to be learning so much. I told her about my first Code Blue, and she told me about a young man who had multiple orthopedic injuries and complex nursing needs resulting from a motorcycle accident. He had on a helmet, so his head injuries were not as devastating as they might have been.

By the middle of the second week, I stopped seeing her when I was coming in. I know now that it was probably because she was coming in at the right time while I was still clueless about my Just-In-Time-ness. Since we worked 12-hour shifts, we weren't always in the hospital on the same days either.

One evening, we left together. I was delighted to see Amanda again and wanted to catch up. She was cordial but not at all talkative. I noticed her scrubs were stained, and her shoulders were not as straight and assured. "Anything exciting?" I asked.

"Oh yeah, you could say exciting," she said as she quickly walked ahead of me. "Have a good night, Kit."

I was a little hurt but decided Amanda must have another place to go after work. We hardly knew one another, after all.

A few days later, I saw her coming in and hurried to catch up before she got on the elevator. "Hi, Amanda. I've missed talking to people my own age. My residency is so different than what I thought. Would you want to have coffee sometime and talk?"

She looked down and didn't answer at first. When she looked up, I noticed deep purple circles under her eyes. Then with a slight smile, she said, "Sure, coffee would be great. Have a good day, Kit." Not waiting for the elevator, she used the stairs to 3 South.

Now I was sure I had done something to upset her. I tried to think of things that had happened in orientation that might have been offensive. Maybe she could tell my residency was rough and didn't want to listen to my whining. All I wanted to do was talk to somebody going through the same things I was going through.

As it turned out, it didn't take long to find out what was up with Amanda. She and I left the building together that night. I was late, as usual; it was almost 8:00 pm. We both said hi. That was the last time I spoke for about 20 minutes.

With a gulp and tears streaming down her cheeks, Amanda said, "I'm sorry I've been so aloof to you. It's just that I hate this. I'm so stupid. I can't get anything right. My mentor says she thinks I'll be OK, but I know she's worried she's got a wash-out nurse on her hands. I make med errors, which is hard to do when the dispensing machine measures out exact doses. Get this! I gave a narcotic to my patient and forgot to chart her response to the medication. That's why I was late tonight. My mentor found it, and I had to go back and document it. Then, the other day, I wasted the proper amount of narcotic but did it alone, and now no one can verify that I didn't take it myself. Once, I cut off a blood band to start an IV. It was in the way of the only good vein I could see! I taped the blood band to the bed but didn't reapply it or report it. So, he needed to have blood drawn again for type and cross match. The lab technician was furious, and the patient got an unnecessary poke."

Then today, I had a patient who was feeling scared about going home, and I missed it. My mentor wants me to do some reading about communicating with purpose. She could have slapped me. I was so surprised. In school, my professors loved my communication notes. You know what? I'm beginning to think that therapeutic communication and empathy and caring and compassion are academic concepts that are "nice to know" but don't have any place in day-to-day nursing. And NCLEX! Passing that doesn't mean anything. Do you know I passed the exam with the minimal number of questions? I thought that meant I knew about nursing.

She sniffed, took a shuttering breath, and then continued, "So, I presume all the NCLEX questions about documentation and communication were answered correctly but have nothing to do with work as an RN. Do you know what I have found out? Almost all my TMH documentation is not up to my mentor's standards, and it seems that all I do is document. The other nurses are always on my back to hurry up. I can't think straight. How do you keep things straight? This is horrible. I'm going to quit. I just have to find another job. Maybe I can work as a school nurse or in a doctor's office or some other easy place. Now I can't even find my car!" She stopped to blow her nose and continued scouting the parking lot.

"How do you stand it? Nobody should have to work this hard. And do I get a thank you from anybody? I mean anybody. No. I do not. All I hear is, 'Honey, would you get me another blanket?' "Nurse, I don't understand why you say my lab reports aren't back yet. Go check again, sweetie.' 'Amanda, have you passed your 10:00 meds yet?' 'Nurse, what was the morning WBC and differential on this patient? Any fever?' How am I supposed to know all this stuff plus give baths, make beds, assess patients, document, and even empty needle boxes? My mentor has bailed me out so far, but it is hopeless. Here's the stupid vehicle. Bye, Kit."

Right then, standing in the parking lot, watching Amanda drive away, I knew I had to get a grip. I knew without any doubt what she meant. I've never worked so hard in my life. This job combines waitress, travel agent, janitor, electronic technician, parent, multitasker, and mind reader. It would have been super nice if they'd mentioned this in school.

On top of all that, we're supposed to simply see multiple facets of every problem, then quickly come up with a correct solution. How could I have been so wrong in my career choice? How could TSU allow me to graduate knowing how bad a nurse I'd be? That can't be true, can it?

I knew I needed perspective. It was almost two months after graduation. I had become a social recluse. The laser focus on nursing and nurse residency had narrowed my social life outside work to mom, dad, and the boys. On my Sundays off, we all trooped to 9:00 am church services. Church is always followed by brunch at the Thompson Diner. We are Lutherans, after all, and brunch after church is de rigueur. Don't get me wrong. The Diner had a great waffle and chicken item to die for. But, other than that, I worked, slept, ate, read up on my patients' meds and nursing standards, dreamed over apartment flyers, and folded down corners in quilting magazines. Then the cycle repeated.

I had to start to get out more. There are people who know me and are also nurses. I felt almost homesick for my days as a student nurse. I needed my TSU suite mates, Mary and Erin. They were both working at the University Hospital and shared an apartment. No childhood bedrooms for them. Their social media commentaries and texts were bubbly and full of funny anecdotes of their nurse residency. They were having such a great adventure. We could compare notes, and they could put me on the right path. Since my Gram lived there, I could see her. Gram is a nurse. She told me the first year was tough for her, and she'd be available to talk. I was sure her views of nursing were outdated (after all, she graduated in 1976!), but she always listened to me. I needed a trip to San Davers. STAT.

I found my car and headed home to make plans with a strategy in place. The weekend before I started on the night shift, I had three days off. I sent Gram and my girls a group text telling them I needed tea (or a decent glass of wine) and sympathy. I wanted to catch up and talk about nursing school versus real-life nursing. Within minutes they all answered my text and said they were available on Saturday for loaded nachos, tea or wine, or both and conversation. Erin said it best. "I miss your face," her text said. "Me too!" we all echoed. After finishing my last week of days, I would set out for San Davers.

Chapter Eight

"**Nursing is a progressive art such that**
to stand still is to go backwards."
Florence Nightingale

B arb and I had established a good working relationship, so Emily agreed she could continue as my mentor until night shift orientation began in week nine. I felt comfortable talking with Barb even when I disagreed with her, so it was good news that I wouldn't have to adjust to another 3 North mentor. I had enough to figure out and adjust to without breaking in a new one.

But first, I had to finish my day shift residency.

The last week of day shift was tough. My workload was increased to a full RN load, and learning multiple new skills kept me on high alert. Then there were Barb's daily summaries. Toward the end, I started to realize that Barb wanted me to succeed. Every day she continued to give me at least one compliment. She called her comments "areas for improvement" and not "criticisms." It didn't matter. They still stung.

That week I took care of a patient that I'll never forget. Anne Blueston was 75 years old. Her husband was Michael, and he made it clear that I was to call them both by their first names, Mike and Annie. Annie was admitted the day before following a stroke. She had not yet gained full consciousness but did respond to commands, such as squeezing my hand and wiggling her toes. She was able to move only on her left side because the stroke had caused right-sided paralysis. Mike never left her bedside. He described himself as an "old hippie" and looked the part. Although he had male pattern baldness, Mike kept a ponytail that went halfway down his back. It was thin and almost pure white. Mike was very forthcoming and loved to talk. He and Annie had been married for 27 years, although they had lived together for over 50 years. "We decided that when the last kid flew the nest, we would make it legal," he laughed, showing even, stained teeth.

Annie had been a potter, and they lived on a small piece of land just outside Thompson that they bought in 1968 after graduating from TSU. Mike grew organic vegetables and sold them to specialty grocery stores. They had had two sons. Both were killed three years apart while serving in the military. "I was a card-carrying conscientious objector during Viet Nam," Mike said proudly. "Not my boys. They joined the Marines. It was peacetime when they joined; then came the war. They were both killed in the Persian Gulf," he quietly said and wiped his face with both hands. "No sympathy needed, nurse. Just thought you ought to know."

The morning before, Annie had fallen at home walking to the bathroom. She was not able to get up, and Mike called EMS. Annie's assessment showed some chronic cardiac problems in addition to paralysis. She was placed on a cardiac monitor. Her heart rhythm was slow or bradycardic, with irregularly occurring episodes of atrial fibrillation. Her heart rate was seldom above 55 beats per minute. Mike explained that Annie had refused a pacemaker and blood thinners a few years ago. She did take a baby aspirin every day but preferred herbal remedies for the occasional aches and pains she felt. "We were vegetarians when it was considered way out there," Mike went on, "We've always lived healthy and didn't see the need for doctors and their drugs. Until now, at least."

On assessment, Annie's skin was pale, smooth, and had no skin breakdown. Her lung sounds were clear on admission, but her breathing was not deep. Annie was at risk for pneumonia and additional blood clots due to bedrest and the atrial fibrillation cardiac rhythm.

I referred Annie to the social worker for early discharge planning. Mike agreed to talk to the social worker but was sure Annie would recover and go home as healthy as she was two days before.

Mike played music on a cassette player for Annie. He played "Blueston's Favorite Hits of the '60s and 70s." The first day I cared for them, I heard John Denver's *Annie's Song* softly playing next to Annie's ear.

> *You fill up my senses,*
> *Like a night in a forest*
> *Like the mountains in springtime,*
> *like a walk in the rain,*
> *like a storm in the desert,*
> *like a sleepy blue ocean.*
> *You fill up my senses,*
> *come fill me again.*

It was hard not to feel a tightened throat and unshed tears watching Mike as he stroked Annie's face and braided her long auburn and silver hair.

The second day I cared for Annie, her condition had slowly improved. She was awake for short periods but was not talking. Radiology studies showed damage to the speech center of the brain. Annie was to have speech therapy when she woke. The social worker had visited and documented, "No social work interventions needed at present; Will continue to follow as necessary." Surely, she was kidding.

Annie and Mike needed some help. I thought I probably needed to take over and plan things for this beautiful, childless couple myself since I couldn't count on the social worker. I cared too much not to start planning for discharge actively.

I was off two days, and then on my last day shift, I learned Barb and I had a different assignment than before. We were not assigned to care for Annie. During report, the night shift RN mentioned that Mike was becoming increasingly worried that Annie was not responding more quickly. "The husband is clueless," she said. "She'll never go home again. He was wondering about herbal remedies." She pantomimed smoking a joint. "Those old hippies don't get it. Brains burned out from crazy living, I guess."

The night nurse's words frosted my cookies. Didn't she read my notes? My admission history? And now I was not allowed to care for Annie?

I was incensed and decided to check in on Annie after report anyway. Suddenly, out of nowhere, the hallway shook with male screaming and high-pitched guitar sounds. I reflexively flattened my back against the wall and even might have squealed.

INAGADDADAVIDA HONEY
DON'T YOU KNOW THAT I LOVE YOU
IN A GADDA DA VIDA BABY
DON'T YOU KNOW THAT I'LL ALWAYS BE TRUE

"Sorry, Sorry, Sorry, Nurses," Mike said as he ran out into the hallway. "Annie used to love to belt that out. She loved Iron Butterfly, and I thought In-A-Gadda-Da-Vida might wake her up! It was set louder than I thought!"

Barb and Lydia Denner, another older RN, burst into laughter, practically holding each other up. "C'mon, Kit, let's introduce you to the early days of acid rock!" They walked me into Annie's room to see her response. The cardiac monitor now showed a sinus rhythm of 72. "That's practically tachycardia for Annie," laughed Lydia. "Mike, you're a wonderful husband and caregiver. Just keep the Top Ten down to a dull roar, OK?"

"OK, Kit," said Barb, "Show's over. Let's get to work."

I was ready to make my pitch for an assignment change. "Wait a sec, Barb. I want to talk with you about our assignment. I have taken care of Annie my last two shifts and know her and her husband. I'm the best person to keep caring for her. Since today is my last day shift, I need to make sure things are in place for them. The night shift report was all wrong about Mike. The bottom line is that I care deeply for them and have a special relationship with them. How can we get the assignment changed?"

Looking a little puzzled, Barb waited a moment and said, "Why don't you think Lydia can competently care for them? What do you have to offer that Lydia doesn't?" Barb paused. "Is it because you believe you care more than she does?"

"Well, care and empathy do go hand in hand," I explained to my mentor. "I want to be sure Annie gets better and goes home. Mike needs to feel the compassion I can bring from knowing them since admission. I should be their advocate."

My logic was smoking hot! I could tell Barb was impressed by the look of amazement on her face.

"Whoa, Kit," Barb held up her hand in a stop gesture, "Tell you what. First, we will get our assigned patients assessed and care for their morning needs. We are not going to request an assignment change. Today, you and I will take a 30-minute break at lunchtime. We need to talk."

I was a little scared, and a lot miffed, but I followed Barb's direction. At 12:15 pm, we met in the conference room with our lunches.

"I'm glad you could get away on time, Kit. I've arranged for RN oversight of our patients while we're in here."

"OK. I'm glad you want to talk. Barb, with all due respect, please hear me out. Caring for Annie is the first time on 3 North that I've felt like somebody appreciated my caring and empathy. Nurse residency has been so busy. I don't feel like I'm making a difference for my patients. That's why I wanted to change assignments this morning," I explained as I opened my lunch. "You know what I mean?"

Barb sighed and leaned across the table. "Oh Kit, let me tell you first that I know exactly how you feel," she paused and softly whispered, "Help me get this right. It's so important."

"Kit, I've found you to be a dedicated and caring person. It shows in your interactions with patients and families. Here's the truth. I'm sorry to tell you this," she said. "Every single nurse I know has gone through the feelings you have. You learned well. Compassion and empathy are the hallmarks of caring in nursing. The trouble is you can't expect a nursing program to teach you in class something that has to be experienced at the bedside. Could we please talk about empathy and caring?"

"Well, sure, that's what I was trying to say this morning," I said. I was incredulous. What is Barb even talking about? I knew about empathy, caring, and compassion and was trying to teach her more about contemporary thinking on these ideas and concepts. Maybe I was too sophisticated in my explanations.

It turns out Barb and I had different ideas. Over the next 25 minutes, she explained that identifying a suffering patient or family member's feelings about their experiences can lead the nurse to action. That's empathy. Barb's definition of empathy was identifying feelings that are causing the patient and family to worry about the future. Action to alleviate suffering is compassion or caring. Small things like calling the person by name, explaining what we're doing or gently turning, and giving skin care to a paralyzed patient are all ways of showing compassion."

She asked me if what she said made sense. I nodded but thought she was wrong because I just knew that compassion and caring required longer relationships with a patient and family than we usually get to give at TMH on 3 North. The reason I'd felt that I could provide this kind of caring was that I knew the family so well. Mike and Annie could tell I cared. Just delivering bedside care was respectful, of course, but not compassionate. Barb must have believed my nod meant understanding because she went on. "Here is something I'll bet they never told you in school. If compassion, caring, and empathy are based on what the nurse wants for the patient or wants the patient to have only one outcome, the nurse could be dragged down in two big ways. You said that you wanted to be sure Annie went home and the situation with her and Mike worked out the way you had envisioned. Kit, you'll set yourself up to become angry or reject patients if they can't or don't do what you recommend. If you feel that your caring is only worthwhile if you are the only one caring for them or your work is good enough only if they get well or follow your advice, then you'll become exhausted."

I nodded, not knowing what to say. "I'm glad you felt comfortable telling me this, Barb. I'm sure I'll find other nurses to help me figure out how to be compassionate even when we're so busy. We should probably get back."

I knew that Barb knew I was brushing her off. But really, how can I be happy in nursing if I don't have control over anything about my patients' health after I take care of them? How would I even know I was making a difference if they weren't better than when they came into the hospital, and I cared for them?

At the end of the shift, Barb and I were going to talk again. This would be a summary or evaluation of my experiences on day shift. I hoped and prayed she didn't bring up what she must think are my shortcomings as a caring nurse. Barb was a good mentor. I learned a lot from her and felt better about being a new RN. My only criticism of her was that I thought her years as a nurse had made her calloused. She probably didn't have many caring or compassionate feelings about people anymore. I hoped I got out of nursing before I got like that.

We had a couple of discharges and an ICU transfer that afternoon. Discharge teaching went well, and both patients thanked me for being so kind before they went home. Somehow, I was able to finish TIMES documentation by 7:00 pm and not have to return to my work after giving report. My organization was spot on today.

Barb was the consummate professional, and her examples and stories about my work helped me see how far I'd come in eight weeks. When we sat down for the summary meeting, I felt uncomfortable for Barb, but she was her typical self. I had a sinking feeling that there was something I was still missing.

We talked about my thoughts and feelings about being a new RN. Barb told me her impressions too. Practicing technical skills such as IV insertion had been satisfying. I was much more confident with each insertion, and using the IV infusion pumps was becoming second nature. A few skills stood out as the most challenging and the most satisfying. One skill was developing an assessment technique that allowed me to keep all my patients' conditions straight in my mind, particularly in TIMES charting.

I felt a little bit less like an imposter and more like a real nurse when caring for my assigned patients. The first week I worked, a family member came to the desk and asked to speak to a nurse. I looked around, and Mary, the unit clerk, softly said, "That's you, Kit." How embarrassing! I didn't believe I was quite a nurse yet. Sometimes part of me still believed that if TMH nursing administrators knew how little I knew, they would never allow me so much responsibility.

An area that needed more work was teaching patients throughout their hospitalization, especially when discharged. Re-admissions can be an important way of identifying whether patients were discharged at the best point in their recovery and if they understood how to keep on the path to recovery at home. If patients are not clear about how to care for themselves when they go home, the chance of re-admission is much higher. There are also financial penalties for the hospital from some insurance carriers if patients are readmitted for the same problem within a set number of days after discharge. Barb suggested I consider that referrals to social work, follow-up clinics, and nurse specialists were a sign of holistic care, not nursing laziness. Working within a team meant that I didn't have to do everything to be confident it was done the "right" way.

Knowing when to ask for help from other nurses was getting easier. But talking to the doctors was a whole different matter. When trying to clearly communicate patient condition changes to physicians, my stomach felt what Barb called "beginners ballet." Two situations stood out.

The first time I spoke to a physician without Barb present, the doctor asked over and over, "What is your concern exactly? Do you have specific information about your concern? Telling me you're concerned or uncomfortable doesn't help me at all!" I thought the man was being especially obstinate and obtuse when I clearly explained that I was worried.

In the second instance, I was determined to be confident and specific. The doctor looked alarmed. "I understand what you're saying about Mrs. Jones. Did I do something to make you angry with the patient or me?" she asked.

Barb came to my aid both times. We practiced the difference between communicating assertively versus aggressively and giving a message clearly versus indecisively. No wonder they emphasize communication so much in nursing school. Some days it seems impossibly hard in practice.

"You'll have opportunities to apply more of these skills on the night shift," Barb said reassuringly. "I don't want to give you the wrong idea about nights. It's not like it's easy. The nurses on nights usually have more actual time than on days to plan. Still, all patients don't sleep at night, emergency department admissions are not uncommon, and night shift nurses have important assignments in documenting quality care and quality improvement efforts on 3 North."

I listened to Barb's advice but was not convinced. The slower pace on nights will give me a chance to relax a little and think about what I've been learning. Reflecting on my practice is an important skill too. That was emphasized repeatedly in the Senior Nursing Seminar and Nursing Leadership courses. I would be able to do that on nights. There's sure as heck no chance for that on days!

The four weeks of 7:00 pm to 7:00 am residency night orientation started the fourth evening after day shift orientation ended. I had a long weekend off, and orientation started at 7:00 pm on Tuesday. Susan was assigned as my mentor. I'd never worked the night shift, so I had only a vague idea of how the hospital functioned in the evening and night. One thing was for sure. Night shift couldn't possibly be as busy as day shift.

Chapter Nine

"Our First Journey is to Find That Special Place for Us"
Florence Nightingale

My weekend tote was packed by 8:30 am Saturday. I was ready to go to San Davers and see my Gram and my former suite mates. As usual, some of the family watched me fold t-shirts and shorts. There is always a sendoff if one of us goes away, even just for an overnight. Don't ask me why. It's the way my family rolls. To be honest, I found it comforting, although sometimes I behaved like a young teenager and acted as though they were all annoying me.

Kai wanted Gram to know that he bought a video game with his birthday money and to tell her it wasn't violent and was suitable for developing problem-solving skills. I rolled my eyes, grinned along with him, and agreed to pass on the message.

Dad and Mom were full of advice. I had let it drop that residency was more complicated than I expected. They were worried about me and didn't know what to say or do to make things better. Consequently, they kept repeating the same general message.

"I know you're a good nurse," Mom said. "I think they are expecting too much of you. You're a loving and caring young woman who has only been out of school a couple of months. They are lucky to have you. Ask your friends about these

12-hour shifts. Those are not good for you. You should work 8-hour shifts like everyone else. It's healthier."

"So you've told me, Mom. A lot. I just need to see and talk to people who know what my job is about and are new like I am."

"Don't let them talk you into quitting and moving to San Davers. You are fine here."

"OK, Mom. I won't let them talk me into quitting."

"Here are the goodies from Weber's Donuts for your Gram. I got her favorites: bear claws and raspberry eclairs. Tell her I said hello and can't wait to see her in a few weeks."

I inhaled the calming fragrance of cinnamon and sugar coming from the still warm bakery box and noticed there were seven in the box. I had been given an apple fritter for the trip.

"They smell outstanding. Thanks for remembering to get a treat for me. Love you."

"Love you more!"

Dad chimed in. "You'll be fine, Kit. Drive safely. Have you got your AAA card? Good. A full tank of gas? Good. I noticed you have about 1700 miles before your next oil change. Tell Gram I'm making ribs for Labor Day, and we're glad she's coming."

"Oh Andy, you know she is trying to stick to a plant-based diet," Mom fussed. "Kit, tell her I'll have plenty of vegan options for her."

I nodded and zipped up my bag.

"Honestly, Vicki, you'd think I was trying to poison my loving mom," Dad laughed and wrapped his arm around Mom's shoulders.

I waved and left them both to their silliness. My gassed-up, properly oiled, freshly washed (thanks, Dad) Civic started right up. I pulled away from the curb, waving at the parents. They were standing on the porch waving as though they had never seen my little red car leave home. I turned on Sirius FM (one of my "Necessary" expenses) and headed for the South freeway. By 20 minutes, cruise control was set, and my apple fritter was half-eaten. My stomach unwrapped, and I took a full deep relaxed breath. It was going to be a good weekend.

Chapter Ten

"If there were none who were discontented with what they have, the world would never reach anything better."
Florence Nightingale

I reached San Davers in about 2 hours. Before going to Gram's house, I decided to stop by the Courthouse downtown and visit my favorite coffee cup magician. Creative Coffees was a charming shop in the middle of the lobby. Abe, whose name badge read "Best Barista, Baby!" greeted me as though I'd returned from the moon. Abe always seemed so happy just to be alive. Getting a latte and conversation from him was like Dijon mustard on a hot dog. It just made the whole thing better.

"I'm here to see Erin and Mary and my Gram," I told him. "What do you recommend for the last part of my journey?"

"Oh, Kit! I can't believe it! You're a real nurse now! I've heard that nurses have a rough job, so you could use one of my special Sunshine lattes with vanilla and coconut milk. I've started putting some dark chocolate shavings on top, and the reviews have been spectacular. It's just the ticket to help smooth the little creases between your eyebrows."

"Oh, don't tell me. Little creases?"

"Afraid so, my otherwise beautiful friend. Don't fret, though. My Sunshine latte, Erin and Mary, and your grandmother will kick those lines to the curb." Abe handed me my latte. "You know, my mom was in University Hospital last month. It was her old neck injury again. The nurses were wonderfully caring. They treated her like a queen."

Before I had a chance to extract from Abe precisely what the nurses did that he found so caring and wonderful, he winked at me and turned to greet the next customer. I took a sip of Sunshine latte and smiled all the way to my car.

Gram lives south of town, and I always make a point to take the route through the historic homes on the edge of town. Ever since I was a little girl until today, when I go by the graceful three-story stone mansions, I think 'someday I'll live in one of those palaces like a glamorous lady.' Gram's neighborhood is only 2 miles farther but was at least 100 years newer and not as stately as most of the Victorians. Her two-story brick and vinyl-sided split level may not be glamorous, but the story of Gram's house is one of my favorite romantic tales.

Gram lives in a neighborhood that was the height of fashion in 1978. Before meeting Gram at a mutual friend's birthday party, Grandpa led a quiet life. He was nine years older than Gram. Grandpa was a successful real estate agent and had been what my brother Teddy would call "an astute saver." They bought the house the month before their wedding when Grandpa got a tip that a previous deal had fallen through. The place was enormous for two newlyweds, but they never regretted it and never moved. "I did work a few extra shifts those first couple years, though," Gram always says.

Gram and Grandpa raised Dad and my Aunt Michelle in that house. They both love to tell the story of how Grandpa came home from a tour of some newly built houses in 1993.

"Well, Jen, I've seen that copper-colored appliances and pale green Formica are not the fashion in the '90s. I know you've wanted to keep the wood paneling in the dining room too, but actually, people are turning up their noses at it." As the story goes, he went on for quite a while, saying that no one had wicker furniture in the living room or glass and chrome tables and mauve wallpaper anymore. They were tastelessly out of fashion.

The story can go on for hours and includes things like an argument over whether to keep or pitch the macrame plant hanger, the hunter green living room carpet, and earth-toned corduroy sofa. The sunburst mirror over the (plaid) sofa was a particular bone of contention. It was one of the last things to go. Today, Gram laughs along with the story, but she didn't give up the décor of her "new" house without a fight. Today, Gram has stainless steel appliances and granite kitchen countertops. The rest of her home is equally up to date. And tastefully so.

But it is her lesson about the reluctant remodel that caused me to remember the house story today. "Don't forget to remember to look at all parts of an issue before you decide. Just because it sounds goofy, or you think it's not for you, doesn't make it wrong. If you think you are the only one who knows how to do something best, that is a big sign that you're on the road to foolish arrogance, not an improvement." Her words sounded suspiciously like Barb's.

Now that I've told you some personal family stories let me tell you about Gram and why I needed her today. Jennifer (Jen) Wilson is 62 years old. She was born in 1956 and graduated from St. Luke the Physician Hospital School of Nursing twenty years later. "We were the Bicentennial class," she says. The diploma nursing school closed in 1983. St. Luke the Physician is closed now. It's called TSU St. Luke's and is part of the TSU Health System.

Gram was a gorgeous young nurse. Her tinted graduation picture shows her proudly wearing the school cap and pin on a white uniform with long sleeves and a round peter pan collar. She has long brown hair swept up under her cap, and her smile is radiant. She has worked as a nurse, either full- or part-time, every year since she passed state board exams and became an RN. Gram went back to school later and received a BSN from

TSU in 2006, three years before Grandpa died. She is a cardiac nurse and has worked at St. Luke's her entire 46-year career. She started in the medical coronary care unit (CCU), then the surgical cardiac care unit (SCCU or open-heart unit), followed by Cardiac Diagnostics, Cardiac Rehabilitation, and the Congestive Heart Failure Clinic (CHF). For the past three years, "and until nursing stops entertaining me and I retire," she has worked part-time in the Quality Improvement (QI) Department coordinating cardiac quality improvement projects. She may be 62, but she reads nursing journals every month and is the smartest nurse I know.

"Kit!" Gram came out of the house and met my car in the driveway. "So glad you're here. How was the drive?"

Gram is so cute. Her blonde-gray hair is cut in a bob, and she never leaves her house without lipstick and mascara. Today, her khaki capris and long tropical shirt would be equally at home at a luau. Did I mention that Gram is a good listener? She never bombards me with questions or information and always makes sure I know that the best part of her day is that I showed up.

"The drive was great. I stopped and got a latte from Abe. It was fabulous as usual, and he says to tell you hi. I'm thrilled to be here." I gave her an enormous hug. "Let me get my stuff. There is so much to tell you and ask you."

I got settled and found Gram in the kitchen with a bowl of fresh raspberries. "Here is a little snack while I get lunch together. I got bagels, corned beef, potato salad, and M&M sugar cookies at Donny's Deli. I'm not as faithful to my vegan diet as I should be! You just sit at the counter and talk to me."

Gram smeared spicy mustard on egg bagels and added a generous serving of warmed corned beef. With a plop of potato salad and a dill pickle, lunch was served.

"Oh Gram, I'm so glad to be here. This is my favorite lunch, you know. Erin and Mary said they'd come by about 6:30. They said they'd like to talk to you too before we go for nachos, if that's alright with you."

"Sure, that's fine. I have a proposition for you ladies, though. I have some pretty delicious sangria and guacamole and sour cream to go with my special Jen's Heavenly Loaded Nachos. Would you want to stay here and talk? There is plenty of space in the family room, and it's quieter than a restaurant. When you're finished with me, just let me know, and I'll go watch one of my Netflix shows in the living room. But. And I mean this. If you'd rather go out, that is perfectly fine too."

I was already texting. "Heck yeah! So much better." came back one reply. "Yes! Sangria and nachos at Gram's!" came the second.

"Well, you have three new and confused nurses for dinner, Gram. I hope you're ready with tissues and advice."

Gram made a pshaw hand gesture and said, "Come on. Let me show you my first quilting project. Then let's get fabric. The owner teaches my beginner's class. She said she'd be there today and wants to meet you. Another nurse from QI is in the class, and I boast about you and your quilting skill all the time."

Oh God help me, I thought. They wouldn't be impressed if they knew what was actually going on with me.

The Sew On and Sew Forth quilt shop in San Davers was long, narrow, and bursting with fabric. On the walls hung a variety of gorgeous quilts. We had a great time talking to Courtney, the owner. Our conversation ranged from quilt patterns, big and small projects, and finding the best expert with a longarm machine to finish the quilt. What a relaxing afternoon.

When we got back, Gram suggested a nap. I fast-walked into my room, kicked off shoes, stretched out on the bed, and woke up an hour and a half later. I hadn't slept that well for almost two months.

Chapter Eleven

"We are becoming a large band. See that we are banded together by mutual good will... Let us give the right hand of friendship."
Florence Nightingale

M y sides hurt from laughing. Gram entertained us with sto-ries of what nursing was like when she was first in prac-tice. Stories of doing CPR kneeling on a bed in a mini-skirted uniform. Stories of "harmless" drugs like diazepam being dis-pensed in large bottles that the nurse measured out for "nervous" patients. Following doctors, while he (almost always he) made rounds, fetching him coffee or juice, making sure there was an empty ashtray at the doctor's side of the nurses' station, and writing down his patient orders for him, so all that was needed was his signature. The most shocking for me was that nurses had to stand whenever a doctor came in the nurses' station and give up her (almost always her) seat for the doctor. "Don't ever doubt that we have come a long way with collegial, not sub-servient relationships, with our physician team members," she said. "Not perfect by any stretch, but a whole lot better." She paused and laughed with more than a touch of sarcasm, "doctors don't smoke at the desk anymore, so we aren't concerned with ashtrays!"

I began to understand why caps, although revered by nurses who wore them and the general public who recognized nurses by them, became an impediment. Gram's story of the first time she was formally disciplined as an RN had Erin, Mary, and me staring at her in open-mouthed astonishment.

"Well," said Gram, as she settled on the sofa with a plate of nachos, "I was floated to the ICU this one day when I was out of school for about two months. I was only given one patient, a young guy still in college. He had a summer job mowing the grass for the county and had been injured while mowing a side bank on the freeway. A piece of a mower blade broke off and entered his leg. The long and short of it is that the wound was deep and developed a serious infection threatening the circulation to his lower extremity. He was in wound and skin isolation. Infection control precautions were on colored cards telling us exactly what to do. This kid was in a private room with an anteroom containing a sink, PPE, and a place for the chart. In those days, the private ICU room was a big deal and was reserved for contagious infectious cases and the occasional VIP Very Important Patient. The colored infection control card's directions told me to gown, glove, mask and put on a pair of plastic eye shield glasses. I dressed up, took off my cap, and went into the room. It was a pretty sweaty hour for me, but he was doing better. I finished my AM care, which is what we called nursing assessment, bath, and bed linen change. After removing all the protective gear and disposing of it in reverse order exactly like the card told me to do, I left the room. I was in the anteroom washing my hands when the supervisor, Mrs. Koplik, came in. She was about 5 feet tall and dressed in spotless white. Her cap was equally spotless and perched on the very top of her head. She never smiled and always made me nervous. 'Well, Miss Mueller, where is your cap?' I pointed it out on the counter and explained that I had taken it off to prevent possible contamination. 'That is ridiculous! How is he supposed to know you're a nurse?' I introduced myself, I told her. "That is not an acceptable explanation," Mrs. Koplik said. An hour later, she returned, showing me that I was written up for insubordination!" Gram paused. "Today, I can laugh about it, but at the time, I was terrified of being fired. There were so many rules that I didn't know, and then I sassed the supervisor to boot!"

"Sassed the supervisor?" asked Erin. "All you did was explain yourself."

"In those days, nurses didn't disagree with supervisors or doctors. I really should have known better. Obedience and respect for superiors were drilled into us in school," Gram said.

"Obedience for superiors? Oh my gosh," Erin whispered.

"Besides that," said Mary. "I want to know how you learned to get on top of everything the patient and family and everybody else wants from you?"

"Well, we had between 16 and 20 hours of clinical experience every week in nursing school," Gram said. "We were supposed to know what we were doing when we graduated. No nurse residency for us. I was ICU charge nurse on the manager's days off."

She looked at each one of us. "You know that while nursing has changed in some ways, in others, it has not. Hospitals know now that BSN graduates need six months to a year to become fully beginner competent. That's why the nurse residency program was started."

"What about patient therapeutic communication?" I asked. "I don't have one single minute to show empathy and compassion. That's what we learned in school was most important."

"Therapeutic communication is a joke," said Mary. "I'm lucky if I answer the questions my patients have about their care. Sitting down to talk about their feelings is not an option."

"Therapeutic communication?" asked Gram with a shocked look on her face. "What do you think that is? A sit-down session with every patient? What has been going on in your minds?"

"It's been so hard to set aside time to talk to patients. I want to show patients that I can empathize, you know, walk in their shoes, and share their suffering. But instead, I'm running around finding things, checking lab reports, passing medications, and helping other nurses. And documenting! Half my day is spent documenting what I just did, I swear."

"All we do is document in the medical record!" said Mary.

"For sure, it's crazy. It never stops. All I seem to do is document in TIMES and answer questions from 10 people at once," echoed Erin.

Gram nodded. "I think I understand. Tell me more."

We told our own stories. I told about Annie and Mike. I still felt that I should have been assigned to them that last day. Gram asked me the almost same question that Barb had: "Why do you think the other nurse couldn't provide a good level of care? What would have made your interactions different from the other nurse's?"

"They could tell I cared for them and wanted to help them. It's a feeling. It's like we were taught. I can't walk in their shoes if I don't spend time with them to find out their problems. It's hard to explain."

She said, "Oh. OK, honey. That's genuinely nice of you. But please keep your own shoes on. The other people's shoes wouldn't fit you anyway. You still help people without long interactions. You learn to focus your interactions on what is needed now and let the person tell you what they understand or what worries them. Listen first. Then address those needs and make sure the information is passed on. As a hospital nurse, you know that you will always care for people and then move on to other patients and families. You can't follow them after you care for them. That's not only inappropriate, but it's also illegal."

I felt embarrassed, as though I had disappointed Gram. I knew that I couldn't follow patients after discharge. I knew patient information privacy was protected by federal law. HIPPA is the law that prevents anyone from accessing a patient's medical information unless they need it specifically to provide health care or bill for services. Did I want to stay involved in Mike and Annie's care even after I left day shift on 3 North? I'd never thought of it that way. There was that focused communication again. The same question kept bugging me: What was I missing?

Erin told a hilarious story about when she was involved in a Code Brown. This is when patients are incontinent, and the urine and stool spread all over the bed and patient. Usually, two nurses are needed to get the person cleaned up. "On this day, I was with my mentor in the middle of the Code Brown, literally up to my elbows in excrement when the senior resident walked in the door. He almost made it to the bed, then slipped and fell on some brown liquid stuff. He kept waving his arms around and making noises and landed on his knees. 'Oh shit,' My mentor said. "Thank heavens the patient isn't aware of her surroundings and is spared this unholy mess."

The rest of the story was anticlimactic but helped me remember to look at the absurd side of health care with a kind eye. Knowing me, I would have probably felt responsible for the poor poopy dude's lack of observation skills. "It's not all about you." Barb's words came back to me.

Mary grimaced and said, "My story is one that I cannot stop thinking about. It was awful. I was awful." Then, she tearfully told the story of how, after report one day, she started down her row of patient rooms in chronological order. "No one had asked me something I didn't know yet that day. I was feeling more confident."

By the time Mary reached her fourth patient, the woman was not responsive. "I should have checked her first. I got my mentor in there. The woman's heart rate was 45, and she wouldn't wake up. I was panicked." Her mentor assessed the patient and identified the problem, supported her symptoms, and STAT paged the hospitalist.

"That's not your fault," I said. "How could you know that would happen?"

"Well, I should have paid attention in report. I had been given plenty of information about how sick she was and how her blood sugars were still not under good control. I didn't think to see my patients according to priority. So stupid! She had to be transferred to ICU. Now my mentor and I are working on prioritizing abilities every day. How could I answer test questions in school about which patients need to be seen first and then completely forget everything in the real world?"

Erin and I moved closer to Mary and held her hands while she talked and cried. What a terrible story.

My hands got cold, and a feeling of actual fear came over me. That could have been me. I didn't make a purposeful point of thinking about what each patient needed right after report. I had been treating my patients' needs like tasks that needed to be checked off until someone told me to hurry up and do something else.

"Organization is the biggest skill you'll learn in the first six months," said Gram. "It can be almost terrifying how out of control things can get. Do you make a list of what's most important before you leave report?"

"There is too much to remember," said Mary. "It seems like everybody needs to be seen right away."

"That old word 'prioritizing' becomes just a natural part of what you'll do eventually, but at first, you need to take just a few seconds after report to decide what needs to be done first, second, and so on." She paused and held up a hand. "I know, the whole plan can go straight to the fifth circle of Hell in the blink of an eye. Whether you've been a nurse for 42 days or 42 years, that is always a risk. The idea is to stop for a couple of seconds and reprioritize as soon as you can."

"OK," said Erin. "But let me ask you this. How do you get all the documentation done for all these interruptions plus the regular assessments and treatments? The older nurses on my unit say that charting wasn't so hard on paper charts. They say it's the EHR, electronic health record that is causing so much trouble with time management."

"Oh man, that's a good one," laughed Gram. "I'll tell you what. Charting has always been a pain in the tail. Always. But it has to be done. You know the old saying, 'If it's not charted, it wasn't done.' Documenting is the only way you can say definitely that you did something, like listen to lungs or turn and position a patient, or anything else for that matter. But paper charting usually required that we write out our assessments long hand. Checklists were considered inadequate for about the first 15 years of my career, so we had to rewrite the same assessment words throughout the day. There were different sections in paper charts too, so don't let anyone tell you that flipping screens is a new torture. There was an Intake and Output section, a Vital Sign section, a Lab results part, Doctor Progress Notes, and other report sections like OT/PT and Surgery in addition to Nurses Notes. Oh, and the EKG monitors didn't automatically record a rhythm strip every day or as needed when set parameters were breached. We ran the rhythm strips ourselves and taped them into the chart…in a separate section of the chart! I wonder what LaLa Land some of my peers lived in before the electronic medical record. Now it's true that we didn't take our charts into rooms in the room and hold the chart in our hands while we were with the patients. The computer medical record on wheels can be an obstacle between the nurse and the patient. But, I'll tell you what. Getting out of work late because we had to catch up on charting was more common than not, even before computers." She paused. "Am I going on and on too much, Kit? Sometimes I don't know when to stop telling my opinions."

"No," we said in unison. "Since you've figured this out, tell us what to do."

"I most certainly wouldn't say I have anything in nursing all figured out, and anybody who tells you that is delusional. Here's what I've decided. The big difference is that in the paper chart days, we would chart what we could remember or what we had written down on our pocket papers. I could have complete information on some charts and not-so-complete information on other charts. But there was nothing that stopped me from being incomplete. Sometimes, somebody would remind me that I didn't chart one thing or another the next day, but I could write what I wanted, sign my name, and close the chart. The chart didn't talk back to us and say, 'Whoo Hoo, you didn't chart the neuro checks!' Now TIMES is a different story. The checklists and notes documentation often have mechanisms built in that prevent the nurse from saving and moving to another section until all required fields are completed. That is a safety and quality check. It can prevent you from making an error of omission because you forgot to chart something. That could save your neck later if legal action is brought, and your name is on that chart. You are so right, my girls; charting is a beast, no question about it. So, stop fighting it. Learn what is on the pages you use and how efficiently to document what's required. You can start to control TIMES. Things will go quicker, and then you'll be in charge, not the software."

The room was quiet. No one had ever defended EHR documentation before except as a not-so-veiled threat that we could be sued and lose our license if we didn't do it right.

"That's enough of me. I've taken up over an hour of your evening, and my Netflix is calling in the other room. No, wait. Hold on. I've got something for you."

Gram left the room and returned with three adorable little books with quilted covers. "Did you know that I keep a journal? I started it when I went back to school for my BSN. It began as an assignment, but I kept it up. There were so many new things about professional philosophy and nursing science that didn't make sense. When I wrote down what frustrated me, I could sleep better and not be as short-tempered with your grandpa. I think I cried less too. Anyway, I mainly wrote down the facts of a situation or whatever was bugging me. Then I went back and reread it a day or two later. Sometimes I added solutions or other thoughts to it. The whole process helped. I still journal every night. The stuff I write isn't overly exciting, but now I like the habit.

"If I could make one suggestion. Since the shifts are so busy, consider taking a few minutes after work or before bedtime to think about what happened that day. Write it down. You might only write down the facts of what happened and how it made you feel. You might write a plan of action for something and come back the next day and see if it still makes sense. There's no special way to do it, and nobody will read it but you."

Erin and Mary and I looked at her. Then Erin and Mary looked at me. I knew what they thought. She was my Gram. I needed to tell her.

"That's nice, Gram. But since I'm out of school, I've decided to give up on writing assignments. Journaling works for some people, but not me. I'm not as touchy-feely as you are." Erin and Mary looked down and nodded.

"Well, that's fine, but please take one. You might try it and see. I'll just let you have them."

I stared at her and tried to look grateful. What's it about the words "I don't want anything to do with a journal," doesn't she understand?

"Well, ladies, that's it for me tonight," said Gram. If you want to come back any time and talk more, that would be great. You are incredible women and will become excellent nurses in our exceedingly complex and confusing health system. And I don't just say that because I'm your Gram and I love you. I'm proud of you." She kissed the top of each girls' head and left the family room.

Leave it to Gram to diffuse the tension. She doesn't seem to realize how humiliating some of these nursing things are for us. She means well, and I love her for it. But why willingly write those horrible incidents down on paper? You can rest assured I'm not going to get started on some journal project.

"' Night Gram," we all said.

"Thanks for the sangria and nachos," said my very polite friends.

"Now," said Erin after Gram left the room. "Let's talk about important things. Ask Mary about the new guy she is dating. How about it, Mary?"

We poured a bit more sangria, refreshed our plate of nachos and dip, and spent the rest of the night exchanging news about our favorite people, places, and events in San Davers.

Chapter Twelve

Reluctant Ruminations

*W*ell, maybe I should be obedient and respectful of my superiors, like nurses were in the olden days of the 20th century and write in this journal. Haha. Nurses didn't have much respect in Gram's day. It was fabulous to see Erin and Mary. They're having the same problems I am. I nearly cried with relief. I needed them so much, and I do feel a little better. Just write down your thoughts, Gram said. OK. Here are some thoughts.

1. Gram's stories were hilarious.
2. I would never have made it if I had to jump out of my seat for doctors.
3. The journal is cute. I like the log cabin quilt pattern on the cover.
4. The journal seems like another assignment I have to complete.
5. I don't like the word journal. It's an overused word that reminds me of a suggestion from psych class. 'Write down your feelings and set your spirit free.' Bah!
6. I suppose I could use it on the night shift and write down my reflections. I wanted to do that anyway.
7. I'll name this journal so that it doesn't seem so school-y. I love alliteration. I like the word Ruminations. I don't want to do this. OK. Reluctant Ruminations is the name.

8. *Probably don't have to number each of these. That looks very school-y. Good Night.*

Good morning. This is the same day, so I'm only going to add to yesterday's Ruminations. I was way too cheerful about all this last night. I must have dreamed mixed up crazy thoughts about last night because I wondered if Gram understood me this morning. It felt good to tell my patients stories and hear from Erin and Mary that they aren't having the day in the sun as their social media posts sounded. But then, Gram, who should have stuck up for me about my views on compassion, instead turned on me. What is the matter with her? I can't believe it.

When I told her how concerned I was about Mike and Annie, she just dismissed my reasons to take care of them on my last day. Very hilarious about staying in my own shoes. Oh, sure, she was nice about it, but why didn't she understand that I just wanted to make sure that I could show Mike and Annie how much I cared? It wasn't fair that I wasn't allowed to care for them on my last day. I know I'm not their nurse anymore. I understand that no one from the family has asked me to care for them or help them. No, I don't think I planned to stay in touch with them after discharge. Yes, the other nurses can show them compassion and concern. But why don't these older nurses get it? I'm not nosey! I care! I was worried! Why does the same message keep coming from the more senior(or should I say more geriatric) nurses? What did I miss in school, or didn't the professors in school know what they were talking about? Were they in an Ivory Academic Tower and sold me a basket full of idealistic crap?

I'm scared that these are signs that I'm not cut out for nursing. Really. Maybe I'm too compassionate to be a nurse. I thought I was going to make a difference. How do the other nurses stand it? It's been a while since Gram got her BSN. She just doesn't understand the new way of giving compassion like I was taught. We are supposed to make the patient feel valued and important. But how to do that all the time makes no sense. If we don't show them how their actions make them sick, how will we help them get well? What don't I get?

What Gram said about paper charting versus EHR documentation was brand new to me. I still despise all the documentation we have to do in TIMES, but I thought documentation used to be easier on paper charts. The annoying stops on the checklists and nurses' notes are safety checks? Sounds a little familiar. Getting more experience with how TIMES works is a good idea. It's about time I controlled something at work. Better to be in charge of a computer program than nothing at all.

And as for no one reading this journal. Did she forget my family shares everything? A journal wouldn't be safe sitting out in my room. You bet your sweet dupa I'm going to hide this. Maybe I'll come back to this later. Maybe.

Chapter Thirteen

"Apprehension, uncertainty, waiting, expectation, fear of surprise, do a patient more harm than any exertion. Remember, he is face to face with his enemy all the time."
Florence Nightingale

I started the night shift on a Tuesday. My focus during the day was planning how to stay awake all night. We never worked past 7:30 pm in nursing school, and my circadian clock is set at early-to-bed-early-to-rise. I never pulled an "all-nighter" in college. It seemed pointless. I can't even watch Game of Thrones or Grey's Anatomy after 11:00 pm. So, to prepare, I took a nap.

It seemed odd to pack a lunch in the afternoon and shower while the sun was out. I didn't take coffee but filled my to-go cup with ice water. "Stay hydrated!" was the advice from more than one-night shift nurse. "Water will keep you awake better than too much coffee."

Barb passed me to Susan as my night residency preceptor. She's closer to my age, and I hoped that maybe she'd be more up to date about newer ways of thinking in nursing. Susan promised she would stick right by me. At least we're on 12 hours shifts, so I have to stay awake only three nights every week.

The hospital lobby was still active with visitors when I arrived at 6:35 p.m. If I learned anything on the day shift, it was to leave home to clock in 20 minutes before the report started. I heard Barb's voice, "At least 15 minutes before the shift begins, kiddo." A first impression is lasting that much I knew from hard-won wisdom as "Just-in-time-Kit."

Susan was already at the nurses' station busily looking at labs in TIMES when I phoned in using the TMH Clock In-and-Out system. Susan Anderson had been one of the first nurses to welcome me on my first day of clinical nurse residency. Although we were still mainly hi-and-bye friends since we've been on opposite shifts, something about Susan's personality made me feel encouraged. She was confident without being a know it all. A couple of times in report, I'd ask a question about something she had already explained, and she never acted like I was stupid. I'm not sure I would have been so nice to someone who obviously wasn't listening or who sounded like they had a super shallow knowledge base. Susan had been out of TSU's college of nursing for seven years. She was 29 years old with a tanned olive complexion. She usually showed a business-like expression, but she had a contagious deep laugh when she found something funny or ironic.

"Hi, Kit. Glad you're here. We've got a few minutes before report starts. Let's get you started on the right foot. The night shift is different in some big ways," Susan said.

She wasted no time. My hands got cold, and I swear I had a PVC or two as the list grew. Patient assignments are greater in number. Staffing is less at night, and there were fewer options if a nurse called in sick. The schedule provides fewer RNs on the night shift than on the day shift. This meant there were 6 RNs on the 7:00 p.m. to 7:00 a.m. shift, compared to 9 RNs on the day shift. The charge nurse for the night shift had a lighter patient assignment than the other nurses but was also responsible for the daily RAD-Q checks and making assignments. RAD-Q was Ready Always to Deliver Quality patient care. It was the quality improvement system at Thompson. Demonstrating correct use of RAD-Q was a competency for my residency. Susan said that two nights would be spent with the RAD-Q nurse next week.

The day shift gave report. I couldn't believe how much the day staff had accomplished. I know I just left that shift, but seriously, there is a lot that goes on in a hospital day. Susan recommended listening in report for changes in condition and tests or procedures scheduled for the following day.

I noticed that Anne Blueston was no longer on the unit. I asked if anyone knew what had happened.

"She was discharged to a rehab facility. That's all I know. Why do you ask?" asked Lydia.

"No reason, Just wondered if we had heard. I took care of her."

"We don't follow patients post-discharge unless they contact us. After we close their chart, it's not our business."

"Right. Thanks." I felt chastised, but Lydia was pleasant. Thankfully, Susan touched my arm and motioned to leave. Her orientation continued.

"We want to see each patient right after report, just like you do on the day shift. We evaluate patients early so that their needs can be anticipated. Of course, we want to avoid unnecessarily waking the on-call physicians and nurse practitioners. Crabbiness is a polite term for clinician attitudes when a phone request after midnight could have been anticipated earlier.

"Let's look at the bedtime or HS medication and as needed or PRN medication orders so we can ask patients about their pain and difficulty sleeping by 11:30 p.m. We want to provide as much uninterrupted sleep for patients as possible. Finally, we want to be sure that we know which patients are required to have nothing to eat or drink after 7:30 p.m. This NPO status has to be told to the CNA we share throughout the unit on our shift. Patients often ask him for a drink of water or snack at night. Placing NPO signs on the door of these patients is one of the tasks that Connor, our CNA tonight, will expect to do. Let's make sure we know which patients will be affected so he can get that finished."

The evening went by quickly. After 10:00 PM, the whole atmosphere of the unit seemed to calm down. Visitors were allowed to stay at night if they chose, but most family members and friends went home.

"We have close camaraderie on our shift," confided Susan. "It's essential for us to be able to depend on each other. Emergencies can happen at night too. When night comes, patients can become anxious. We can be surprised by quietly sleeping patients whose condition suddenly deteriorates and patients who worry that they are going crazy because they feel afraid after dark. That is another reason we thoroughly assess our patients early in the shift. Very grown-up people frequently ask for the light to be kept on. The first time a big man who looked like a football player and was in his 50's asked me to keep the bathroom light on, I started to understand why we want to make hourly rounds when we can."

After 1:00 a.m. rounds, I was completely caught up. My assessments and medications were documented, there were no medications to pass, and our assigned patients were sleeping or at least resting. Now, this was more like it—nothing to do. I was mentally patting myself on the back. Nurse Organization here! I could get used to this pace and told Susan. "It's so nice that there's nothing to do now until a light goes on. Do you bring a book to read or something?"

Susan and another nurse, Deb Hillman, standing nearby, leaned against the wall and laughed. Their chuckles were soft, but when they looked at each other and said, "Oh yeah, right," I knew that, once again, there was something I didn't get.

Susan was nice. She put her hand on my shoulder and put on a straight face. "I love that you think there is nothing to do. It has been pretty routine and quiet for you so far tonight. We tend to have more free time than the day shift, but some nights are every bit as busy. When I have a lull, I try to ensure the other wings are doing OK and help out if needed. Tonight, we are lucky to have the chance to get to know each other. I'd be happy to review charts with you too. It will help keep you awake, and you can learn more about nursing care for our patients."

I smiled and inspected my nails. Oh yeah. Being quizzed by an experienced nurse is exactly what I hoped to do on nights. No, thank you!

Deb and Susan explained that my mistake was quite common among people that didn't work nights. It was hard to understand that some essential things were apparent only when they weren't completed; many of these tasks were assigned to the night shift. This allowed the unit to maintain the highest quality of care. For example, at TMH, the night shift staff were responsible for patient medication reconciliation and validating expiration dates on stock foods and sterile supplies. Progress toward patient discharge goals was evaluated and reported every morning by night RNs.

"We're not laughing at you. Please don't take offense," said Deb. "We're laughing at how easy it is to misunderstand the quiet and calmness. Organization is critical since we don't have as many RNs to care for the unexpected, like when new admissions come or a patient's condition suddenly deteriorates. The only expected thing on nights is that the unexpected usually happens."

Deb paused and went on, "When I first started on nights, it took a while to understand these two sides of the same coin. You know, we have to stick to a routine while preparing for the unexpected purposefully, yet we also have to make the environment as peaceful and low-lit as possible so that patients can rest. We don't rest, but we create the environment of rest," she concluded.

Susan nodded and said, "Making the environment quiet to promote healing sleep is such a nursing priority on nights. Come on, Kit, let me show you what we do instead of reading books!"

We reviewed the expiration dates on the crash cart medications and the nutrition supplements. We verified the number of wheelchairs we had and that they had been cleaned and worked well. We reviewed our assigned patients' goals for discharge and identified who may benefit from referrals to hospital and community services. Diabetes Educators and the Heart Failure Clinic were probably the busiest outpatient services. I had to do a mental head slap when we counted wheelchairs and sent stretchers back to their homes in OR, ED, or Radiology. Who did I think did these checks? The equipment gnome? That was the first time I realized how purposeful action behind the scenes affects quality nursing care.

We did have time to talk a bit. Susan was sympathetic about my adjustment to adult finances. "Everyone here has gone through money shock. Talk to us. We'll tell you what to do! Nurses have an opinion about everything!"

Susan and I did have some things in common. We're both beginning quilters and talked about signing up together for a quilting class in the Fall.

Connor appeared around the corner. "Susan, Mr. Philips is having a tough time. He is restless and can't get comfortable. I've given him a back rub and straightened his sheets. Could you look at him?"

Susan got right back to business. "Let's go look. The first thing we will do is check out Mr. Philips' physical condition. He has a foley catheter and an IV. Since he has only been out of ICU for a few hours, several things may be going on."

Susan introduced me and asked, "Can you tell us what's going on, Mr. Philips? Are you having pain from your heart surgery incision?"

As they talked, Susan evaluated the urine drainage from the Foley catheter and made sure Mr. Philips' IV was infusing properly. She listened to his lungs and reviewed his cardiac monitor reading.

"No, I'm not in pain, and my dad's name is Mr. Philips. I'm Josh. I just can't get comfortable. I keep thinking about how far away you nurses are. In ICU, I could always see a nurse. Plus, you know it's not a good thing for me to be in the hospital. It doesn't look good that I'm in the hospital. The company I work for always plans for lay-offs at the end of the summer. They'll think I can't work hard."

Susan looked over at me and raised her eyebrows to indicate, "go ahead." I had no time to think but sat down next to Josh's bed. Finally! A chance to communicate directly with a patient about his concerns! So far, I loved the night shift.

"Wow, Josh, no wonder you can't get comfortable. You've got a lot on your mind. I have a few minutes right now to sit and talk with you. You know it's true that worries seem bigger at night. You're worried that you'll need a nurse, and we won't know. And on top of that, thoughts about work are bugging you," I said using reflection of feelings.

"That's exactly right. It's like the devils have come out tonight."

Josh Philips talked on and on about his job and the unexpected surgery to repair a heart valve. The words Open Heart Surgery had scared him the most. He kept waiting for his monitor to alarm because his heart had stopped like on the medical shows. Even though it was noisy, the ICU was a comfort to him, and the lights were on day and night. Slowly I was less stiffly erect in my chair and began to carefully listen to what Josh's primary concern was. I could tell he was nervous and felt unsure, but I hoped to find out what he was most worried about now that he was out of ICU.

Josh didn't know that more than one nurse was around at night on 3 North. When things became quieter, he thought everyone went home, leaving only one or two people at the nurses' station. Josh knew where the call button was located and could reach it. He'd not ever used it, so I encouraged him. Both of our pocket pagers rang. A voice came through the intercom, "May I help you?"

"See Josh," I told him, "We are only a push button away if you need us. You're not alone. Also, we quietly come around every hour or so just to make sure you're OK. If you're sleeping, you'll never know we're here."

After 10 minutes, Josh yawned and said, "I'm getting tired. Thanks for your advice. It helped."

I was thrilled with how this turned out. At last. A successful communication experience for me. It was embarrassing to remember my day shift communication missteps.

"You're welcome, Josh. Sleep well."

Susan patted me on the shoulder after we left the room. "Well done, my friend. Communication is such an important and tough thing to learn." I shivered with relief.

Lunch is between 2:00 am and 4:00 am. The cafeteria is closed on nights. Leaving the unit would have been tricky anyway with so few nurses. We took turns taking 15-minute breaks and eating in the conference room. That first night I was congratulating myself on such a great lunch. I know bologna and cheese spread isn't the healthiest, but I love it! The raspberries and carrots made up for it, maybe.

My pager signaled. Miss Sylvia Smith in Room 330 needed assistance. The small elderly woman in the bed smiled toothlessly and asked to be helped to the bathroom. I walked the slight and bent Miss Smith to the toilet. She carried herself with dignity and insisted on putting on her robe and matching slippers for the short trip. I stayed outside the bathroom door, then walked her back to her bed, removed her slippers and robe, straightened the linens on the bed, and placed the call light within reach. "What else can I do for you?"

"Well," she lisped, "You have pretty hair and are a nice nurse. You have studied very well. I can tell these kinds of things since I was a librarian for over 40 years." I smiled and waited.

"I feel it behooves me to tell you something important that you may not be aware of, my dear. . After all, knowledge is not the only important attribute for those of us who work closely with the public." She touched my hand and looked earnestly in my face. "You have very bad breath."

My face flushed immediately, and I think I gasped. "Oh my gosh, Miss Smith. I'm so sorry to have offended you. Thank you, though for letting me know."

"That's OK," she closed her eyes. "We girls have to stick together."

I found my purse and a breath mint and considered telling Susan. Nah. I didn't need to embarrass myself twice that night.

After reporting to the day shift, Susan walked me to my car. "I know the first night shift is often easier than the next ones because you're not overly tired. You don't know how tired you are, though, so here's my final tip for tonight. Drive with your air conditioning on full blast, play the radio, and sing. Don't talk on the phone. Drive safely. See you tonight."

Chapter Fourteen

Rethinking this Journal Thing Ruminations

Here's what I had figured out so far on nights. #1. Get over those two patients I wanted to care for before leaving days. (no names or identifying information here...because HIPPA.) 2. Admit I was maybe not entirely correct to have insisted that my caring was better than any other RN.

I had an incredibly excellent communication opportunity tonight. But even if there is time to sit down and talk, it's not as easy as it sounds to communicate with compassion and empathy to someone scared or worried. I didn't know what to say to my patient, so I didn't say much. It turns out that just closing my mouth and listening worked. The key is figuring out what that person thinks is the problem or bad thing that will happen. I had not given Josh any advice but just stayed with him and listened to his worries until he could tell me what thoughts caused him anxiety. Then, I tried to reflect those feelings to him. No one was more shocked than I was when Josh told me that he had figured out how to cope with his worries. Mainly, I just sat there and listened. In nursing school, they called it presence. Well, presence made a difference tonight.

Note to self: Tonight is the end of garlic bologna or any other smelly food for my work lunches.

Chapter Fifteen

"The craving for 'the return of the day', which the sick so constantly evince, is generally nothing but the desire for light."

Florence Nightingale

It took until the first weekend night shift before I felt the effect of turning my schedule upside down. I worked two nights in a row, then had two nights off. It was not such a big deal, I thought. I was fatigued and stayed up half the night on the first day off, but everything was normal. I then worked one night and had a night off. The following week was one night shift and two days off. Easy peasy.

I got out my sewing machine and completed quilted placemats as an "I appreciate you" gift to Barb on my days off. I even made dinner one night! My high school friend Hannah and I met for a late lunch one day. Poor thing had to go back to work afterward.

The thing I liked best about the days off after the night shift was that I could think about the patients I cared for and the nurses working with me. I was feeling pretty darn good about my progress.

Then came the weekend. Night weekends at TMH are Saturday night and Sunday night. By Sunday morning, I felt like I was hit by a train. My circadian rhythms were completely thrown off. I slept almost eight hours during the day and still was tired and dull-witted. After a few hours' sleep, I was wide awake, slept for another five hours, then dragged myself into the shower at 5:30 pm.

I dreamed about my patients and made horrific mistakes in my dreams. Susan and Barb came to me in one dream and said, "I'm sorry, Kit, you can't be a nurse. You aren't smart enough or compassionate enough." I woke up at 10:15 am in horror, then relief, and I passed out again.

Between shifts, my big plans to reflect on my practice became absurd. I could hardly decide whether to do my hair in a sloppy bun or a ponytail. It was a good thing I didn't have to pick out an outfit to wear. God bless scrubs. By the time I got to work, I was pretty wide awake. Then Pow! By 2:00 am. I was so overcome that I could have fallen asleep while turning and repositioning a patient. At almost 4:00 am, I popped wide awake.

The night shift was wreaking havoc on my social life, my eating life, my sleeping life, my whole life. After shift report at 7:30 am, I found that I was ready for a huge diner breakfast but was a party of one. My non-night shift friends were already at work in their regular jobs, and all my night shift colleagues had little kids at home.

I was constantly cold in the middle of the night. The thought of eating at 3:00 am had become nauseating. I wanted a bowl of oatmeal, and the other nurses were eating full-course lunches. I was losing weight, and every evening the ties on my scrubs needed to be cinched tighter. How was I supposed to do a month of this? The other nurses assured me that this was all normal. It took more than a few weeks to fully adjust to the night shift.

Susan gave me helpful suggestions. I brought a sweater to work and made nearly constant rounds when real tiredness set in. My lunches were light and mainly nutritious; I always brought a small candy bar or two. After our patients were assessed and documentation completed, I made a point of telling the other nurses I was available to help. That turned out to be a brilliant idea. Not only did I endear myself to the other night nurses who

I helped, but I also got the chance to start a couple more IVs, reinsert a nasogastric tube and review a complicated patient's laboratory results with Susan.

By the end of my third week, I realized just how tightly staffed the unit was on the night shift. If a night nurse called in sick, there was no guarantee that a float nurse would be available since all units were tightly staffed.

Talk about having precisely the number of needed staff every night! There was no wiggle room. Susan told me that she knew Emily Smith was aware of the fundamental problems of budgeting for safe staffing on 3 North. I never realized when I was in school, but poor staffing is one of the most common reasons nurses say they leave bedside nursing. The best-laid plans for keeping adequate staffing every single shift regardless of days off and call-ins don't always work.

The last two staff meetings I attended discussed the idea of every 3 North staff nurse taking a few on-call shifts each month to ease staffing crunches. If more nurses were needed because of sick calls or patient acuity, the on-call nurse could be called in to help. These on-call shifts would be scheduled on nurses' regular time off. There would be an incentive: nurses would receive an hourly on-call pay stipend even if they were not called in. So far, it was not a popular option with the 3 North RN staff. Although nurses on 3 North were committed to supporting each other, their days off were highly valued.

Susan was the charge nurse this night. We had the correct number of nurses working that night. According to the staffing plan, Susan would be assigned five patients, make unit assignments, and complete the RAD-Q (Ready Always to Deliver Quality) nursing checks.

Like all hospitals with national accreditation, an annual quality improvement plan was in place throughout TMH. Every unit completed some parts of the plan, and some parts of the plan were unit specific. The data were collected every day, usually on the night shift. By looking at a few particular indicators in key areas, it was possible to show nursing administration and national accrediting associations how TMH monitored and improved care to meet the most current quality patient care standards.

This month on 3 North, the RAD-Q checks focused on proper care of glucose monitors for diabetic patients and daily weights recorded for all those with a medical diagnosis of heart failure. Quality checks are a more sophisticated aspect of nursing care. I enjoyed learning RAD-Q. It also helped me stay awake with less angst.

By the last week of the night rotation, I started to think that maybe this part of the residency would end without problems. I should have remembered Deb Hillman's words, "The only expected thing on nights is that the unexpected usually happens."

Chapter Sixteen

"I attribute my success to this – I never gave or took any excuse."
Florence Nightingale

From the moment I arrived, I could tell something was wrong. The day shift had had two admissions from the Emergency Department and one ICU transfer. One of the day shift RNs called in sick as well. A float nurse came down from Pediatrics to help, but he did not know the 3 North routines.

The night shift had one nurse call in too. Susan quickly assessed the situation and made some decisions. Five RNs, one CNA, and one nurse resident RN were on duty. I was assigned to work as a float nurse between the wings. I was to assist, as requested, with assessments, medication administration, and perform needed procedures. I wasn't under Susan's direct supervision but would work as an extra pair of professional hands. After meeting the patients' needs, we would complete the RAD-Q checks.

"I've talked with the other nurses. We could give you a full assignment tonight to compensate for the short staffing. However, you are still pretty new. We've decided you will serve as a float RN within the unit and help the others. I want you to be open to their requests and ask for clarification as needed," said Susan.

We were busy throughout the evening with assessments and procedures. The large patient load brought home the importance of safe staffing levels. I was glad Susan made me the float and had not assigned me my own wing. That night I asked so many questions from all the nurses since I didn't have Susan to share the assignment.

At 11:30 p.m., Susan said, "Let's plan to do RAD-Q checks in an hour." I hustled to all the other nurses to see if they needed help and met Susan at 12:30 am.

Susan showed me where to look for the data in RAD-Q and double-checked my findings. Tonight, the charts were 100 percent accurate.

While Susan and I reviewed the RAD-Q glucose monitoring quality checks, Susan's pager rang. A patient from the Emergency Department was to be admitted to our last empty bed.

It seemed like seconds after the phone call that Mr. John Jackson, the transfer from the ED, was at the unit's door accompanied by Emergency Department staff. Mr. Jackson was a 27-year-old man driving home on a rural road from a poker game with his friends when a deer ran out in front of his 20-year-old truck. He swerved, hit the tail of the deer, and came to a stop in a field of soybeans. His truck didn't have airbags, and X-Rays showed a large bruise on his chest where the steering wheel hit him. He had bilateral fractured wrists and a broken collarbone. No rib fractures were seen on X-Ray. John admitted he'd had "a couple beers" during the poker game. He agreed to a blood alcohol test. The results were low enough to rule out intoxication at the time the blood test was drawn.

I was assigned to admit John. His lung sounds were clear and equal, and he didn't have any trouble breathing despite the large bruise on his chest. His pulse oximeter reading was 99 percent which was excellent. Pain had been well controlled in the Emergency Department. A continuous IV medication pump was connected, and he reported a 3 out of 10 pain level. The orthopedic surgeon would visit in the morning. Splints held both wrists in anatomical position. Circulation checks on all extremities showed strong pulses and pink color. All bruises and abrasions were examined, cleaned, and their condition documented. His wife arrived with a sleepy toddler in tow, looking worried. She seemed to understand what had happened and, except for telling him he was a "stupid ass," settled quietly with the little boy in the room's recliner.

Following report to the day shift and giving Emily Smith the RAD-Q documentation, I walked out with Susan yawning. "I didn't even have a sleepy time tonight," I said. "That must be the trick. Stay busy, and you'll stay alert."

Susan nodded. "Short staffing from sick calls and unexpected admissions can make it hard to keep everything straight. Let's talk tonight...your last night...about ways to hold it together when things get super busy."

I followed my singing routine going home. I'm not sure how I got out of my clothes and into a long t-shirt, but I was asleep the moment my head hit the pillow.

Chapter Seventeen

Reflective Ruminations

It's almost time for my 3-month evaluation. One-half of the way through residency. The evaluation procedure at TMH is a detailed one. I was asked to complete a self-evaluation. The self-evaluation was an online form divided into categories corresponding to the RN job description and TMH's mission. Writing the self-evaluation was sobering. Remember the first day when I suggested an utterly wrong medication during the code? Barb was very patient with me. It took me almost two months to understand how much I needed to listen and then ask for clarification rather than suggest what I thought I'd learned in school. Not only Barb, but Susan and the rest of the staff here have years of experience. If anything, the self-eval showed me once again that I had a whole lot to learn. Learning never ends in nursing. That's one lesson from nursing school that I got right.

I was lucky to be assigned to born teachers as mentors for day and night shift residency. After sending my self-evaluation electronically to Emily, she and my mentors would use it and add their evaluation notes to complete the official 3-month evaluation. We would talk about what I did well, what I was still in need of improving, and whether I had passed the requirements to go on to the second two months of residency.

If my evaluation was satisfactory, then on Tuesday, I would begin a two-month residency rotation in the Intensive Care Unit.

On my way out a couple of weeks ago, I told Emily that I had submitted my self-evaluation. I must have looked as unsure as I felt because she got up from her desk. "I've been a manager on 3 North for a few years now, Kit," she said, "and I know these evaluations are scary. I can promise you; there should be absolutely nothing new or surprising in your evaluation. We want to give you a united summary so you can move ahead with more confidence."

Like a blithering dip, I said, "You said I was moving ahead. Oh, thank you, thank you, Emily."

She chuckled, patted me on the shoulder, and told me to have a restful sleep.

Chapter Eighteen

"Nursing is an art: and if it is to be made an art, it requires an exclusive devotion as hard a preparation as any painter's or sculptor's work."
Florence Nightingale

My last night shift ended on a Friday morning. After morning report, I had an appointment to meet with Susan, Barb, and Emily to review my 3 North residency evaluation. At that meeting, a written evaluation from my mentors would be given to me.

The meeting was pleasant. Emily ordered coffee from Dietary, and Barb brought cookies. Although Barb and Susan had talked with me during residency about my tendency to correct my peers with "the way I learned it in school," at first, I didn't get it. I thought I was helping the staff learn the latest knowledge, and then they would see that I fit in. Sometimes I wonder if I had the reasoning ability God gave geese. Such arrogance! I understand now that when I "corrected" staff, communication was interrupted. Staff members pulled back, and I didn't learn as much as I might have about how to transfer school knowledge to patient care.

"It's not that you were necessarily wrong, Kit," said Emily. "It's that often listening to the whole message is helpful. Then, rather than thinking of a way to correct a colleague, ask if your thinking is right."

Barb had this unnerving tendency to read my mind. She knew I was wondering how I was doing compared to what they expected for a nurse with my experience level.

She said, "I want to be sure you hear us say how well we believe you are progressing. Your technical skills, such as IV starts, have become quite proficient. You are an empathic nurse. Communication skills with patients are coming along nicely. Some of your colleagues have commented to me on how well you explained procedures and made patients and families feel safe in the hospital."

"Just one more thing that made a difference in how well you're prepared every day," Emily continued. "I know we talked about this a long time ago, but since it's your final residency evaluation, this needs to be mentioned and documented," she paused and smiled. "Your timekeeping is nearly the best on 3 North. Well done. Keep it up."

Susan chimed in, "Speaking of TIMES, your documentation is quite complete, especially for your stage of professional development. When you came to nights, there was some concern that you were at war with our electronic record. I don't know what happened to correct this, and now you're approaching documentation systematically and accurately. That's a big deal, and I wanted you to know it's recognized."

Thank you, Gram, I thought. You got me out of the boxing ring with TIMES.

Then it was my turn to respond. "Yes," I said. "No more Just in Time Kit! You've all helped me through some humbling awkwardness during these past three months. Thank you for understanding because I want to be a good nurse. I enjoy nursing most of the time and especially 3 North. I wanted to tell you that I saw Mr. Koncel in the grocery a few days ago. His cart had only fresh fruits and vegetables and lean poultry in it. We had a nice chat. He thanked us over and over and praised the cardiac team at TMH. I have to tell you I felt proud to be a nurse at TMH, and I stood a little straighter going home."

The nurses smiled and nodded. "It does give you a good feeling when a patient is discharged and is doing well. The Thompson community is so small that we frequently run into people we've cared for. It's not being a braggart to say that it's great to be part of the most trusted and respected profession in the U.S. Nurses work under physically demanding conditions and have to be ready to analyze assessments every minute we're with patients. It can be tough to keep it all straight and put on a professional face all the time," said Barb.

Susan agreed, "You hit it on the head, Barb. I can't think of a better team to work with either. You'll have some complex experiences in your next rotation in the Intensive Care Unit, Kit. Anytime you want to talk, we're here for you. We'll be here when you return for your last month of residency."

"Don't forget to take care of yourself too," chimed in Emily. "What are your plans outside the walls of TMH?"

"Well, I have a long weekend starting today before the ICU rotation starts. I've made a promise to myself to start yoga again tomorrow. A high school friend and I are going to a class in the morning. My biggest goal outside work is to find the perfect apartment. I'm a little picky in my choices. My brother tells me I have Saks 5th Avenue expectations on a box store budget. I'm saving like a wild woman to have enough cash to make it happen. Mom and dad are great letting me stay with them, but I want my own place. Thanks for telling me your stories about the astonishment of take-home paycheck amounts after the deductions. At first, I also forgot to factor in internet and utilities…and ….renter's insurance… Oh my gosh. It's expensive."

The other women burst into laughter. "Oh yes, and don't forget you have to eat. That's right. Paychecks are never big enough. Nurses are paid well, but none of us is going to get rich doing our work," said Barb.

Driving home, I was filled with gratitude for the 3 North evaluation. I hope someday I can help a new nurse as much as Susan, Barb, and Emily have helped me.

Mom made one of my favorite meals tonight to celebrate the successful completion of the first part of the nurse residency. Her clever theme was "Successful Beginnings." It's actually just breakfast (the beginning of the day) for dinner (the successful conclusion of the day.) Get it? Pancakes and omelets and bacon and rye toast and yogurt with fruit. This residency is helping me appreciate the little things in life.

Chapter Nineteen

Relieved Ruminations

*O*ne thing is for sure about nursing. Nothing is for sure. I keep learning little pieces. I'm not as blind as three months ago, but do I understand it? Hell no! (My language is getting more and more curse-y during residency.) I wonder if Gram can see the whole picture of nursing. She is sure to have an opinion, and her opinions have saved my behind more than once during nurse residency! I'll ask her next time.

The nurses and other staff I have worked with so far at TMH have taught me a lot. Some characters are working here, that's for sure. A lot of them have views that are a universe different from mine. Deb on nights has been a nurse for almost 20 years. On nights, Margaret Mary (I keep thinking she's a nun with that name) has to be one of the oldest RNs I've ever met. I'll bet she's older than Gram. I love it when the other nurses talk about the "good old days" when documentation was done on paper charts, and nurses wore caps so that "at least patients knew who a real nurse was." I guess they didn't have big enough name badges in those days! Gram, bless her heart, helped Erin, Mary, and me get a less negative perspective on that stuff. Oh, and Tanya! She's my favorite CNA even though she tells me all the time, "I am practically an RN because I've worked here so long." Thanks be to my mentors and the expert Code Team too!

But my evaluation was pretty good, right? I think I get it now: Nursing residency is a lot of learning, but I think I can handle the next step after these three months. Intensive Care Unit nurses have fewer patients, only one or two. Plus, the patients have monitors that will tell me if there are problems. I'll review EKG rhythm strips this weekend. Bring it on ICU!

Chapter Twenty

"It is a much more difficult thing to speak the truth than people commonly imagine."
Florence Nightingale

The yoga teacher serenely smiled, placed her hands in a prayer position over her heart, and bowed to the group. "May the light in me reflect and respect the light in you. Namaste."

Standing in my yoga pants and TSU t-shirt, I stood tall and responded to the yoga teacher's respectful farewell. "Namaste." Class over. I sighed and stretched again.

Turning to Hannah Greenberg, my BFF from high school, I couldn't help grinning until my cheeks stretched. "I needed that! Why didn't you remind me earlier to come back to yoga? I might have tolerated some of the night shift without so much kicking and yelling!"

We rolled up our mats. Hannah looked serious. "Our lunch was nice a few weeks ago, but too quick. It seems like you've been in a shell all by yourself since you moved home. I finally decided to call you and see if I could make an appointment on Nurse Kit's busy calendar. Missed you so much, buddy!"

When Hannah called, I was ready to do more. Returning to yoga was the first step. Hannah and I have been best friends since she and her mom moved to Thompson from the suburbs of Detroit, Michigan when we were in the 7th grade. Jackie Greenberg, Hannah's mom, opened Thompson's first (and still only) antique and consignment shop.

When we graduated from high school, both of us went to TSU. Hannah majored in Interior Design, so we hadn't seen much of each other for the past few years. We both moved back "home," and Hannah worked with her mom in the shop. She had plans to offer design services for customers with an eye for antiques and style through the shop.

The yoga studio is conveniently placed next door to an ingenious combination business. While we were in college, Hazel's Coffee and Tea Shop and The Best Cookie Company merged. They kept their individual names but share an old storefront downtown store and have the most skilled baristas (except for Abe in San Davers, of course) and the best dessert bakers in the Midwest. Talk about the convenience of one-stop shopping! I got our lavender tea lattes, and Hannah stood in line for the black and white cookies.

"So," we said in unison.

"What's been going on?" Hannah finished.

For the next hour and 20 minutes, we monopolized a corner table. Hannah told me her marketing ideas for interior design services. She had offered staging services to real estate agents so properties look chic and appealing to potential buyers. Hannah had staged three houses so far between her mom's consignment inventory and occasional antique piece and flea market finds. Each of them sold within ten days, so she was pumped. Her creative ideas were endless, and listening to her was energizing. For some reason, hearing about color variations, room arrangements, and life balance through feng shui made me happy. We didn't talk about blood cultures, care priorities, wound healing, or anything nursey.

My cookie was gone and my latte cup almost empty when Hannah said, "Enough about me. How's nursing? Is it fun?"

Fun? No. Terrifying? Yes. Exhausting? Yes. Sometimes affirming? Yes. Intellectually challenging? Oh, Yes indeed. I tried to explain what it has been like learning to practice nursing. How I don't know enough and can't always connect pieces of patients' needs yet and how I'm frequently wrong, or at least not correct enough. How scared I was most days. How I felt like I didn't know what I was getting into when I graduated from nursing school.

Hannah nodded, laughed, smiled, and frowned at the appropriate places in my rant.

"We'd better go before they start to charge us rent for the table," I said. "I need a shower." We hugged and promised to do this again on my next Saturday off.

Walking to my car, I felt lighter, and my shoulders weren't as squinched up. I'll never forget this day with Hannah. That Saturday, I recalibrated and reset my mind's attitude. Switch-it-up Saturday.

Chapter Twenty One

Recalibrating Ruminations

I don't think I did a particularly good job explaining to Hannah what was behind my feelings about what nursing was turning out to be like versus what I thought it would be. It was hard to describe. While I looked forward to going to work, I wondered every single day if I had what it takes to practice as a nurse safely.

Hannah did what every good friend does. She reassured me that I was better than I thought. The people that corrected me just didn't understand. I was a good nurse. I just had beginners' jitters. Things would get better. She was sure of it.

Hannah did do me a big favor, although she didn't know it. She reminded me that self-care is no joke. Nurses can't forget time for exercise, friends, and delicious snacks. At the risk of sounding like a fortune cookie insert, you really can't help people get perspective on their health if you can't get equilibrium in your own life. I'm not sure how to pull that off for the rest of my life, but I know it's important. No doubt. Who has the time? Who has the energy? Figure it out, Kit Wilson!

Today's bottom line is this: I needed to hear the fake reassurance Hannah was giving me. She didn't understand, but she was on my side. That was good enough for now, on the eve of my ICU residency. Breathe in, Breathe out. All is well.

Chapter Twenty Two

"Far the greatest things grow by God's law out of the smallest. But to live your life, you must discipline it."
Florence Nightingale

I went into ICU orientation with a positive attitude. I was determined to work hard, work smart and learn in a disciplined fashion. No more would I let events of the day control me. I would communicate closely with my mentor. I would study what I didn't understand. I would be better than just fine, thank you very much.

I always felt better in nursing school if another student was assigned to the same unit. Painful, as well as good clinical experiences were better shared. Amanda Milton and I were scheduled to be in ICU orientation together. I had not seen her since the day of what I think of as *the parking lot meltdown*. I did send her a message a couple of days after that saying, "Thinking of you and hope you're feeling better about nursing."

She responded, "Thanks. I'm working through it."

Did that mean she was going to be with me on Tuesday? I had to know. It seemed there were three possible scenarios for Amanda and ICU orientation. One, she was still in the residency program, and I would see her in ICU; two, she was repeating some of the first two months to get more experience and would orient to ICU at a later time; or three, she had left TMH for greener pastures. I have had enough surprises at work in the last three months. Yesterday, I sent her another message saying,

"Looking forward to being together in ICU orientation." Late last evening, I got a response, "I'll be there."

I needed to use my employee ID badge to access the doors to the ICU. Only those staff with permission from Security were allowed to enter the ICU with their ID badge. A doorbell can be pushed for visitors and others who need clearance to enter the ICU.

Last week I was sent a lengthy email from Lucy Becker, the ICU manager, saying she had notified Security to give my name badge four-week access to the ICU doors. Lucy's note explained that locked doors are important in ICU to allow staff uninterrupted time to address the near-constant demands of caring for critically ill patients. Visiting hours are scheduled, making it possible to make sure visiting policies are followed (generally, only immediate family members over the age of 12) and every visitor washes their hands on entering. Nurses know that ICU visitors need communication and information too. Scheduled visitation sets aside time predictably for the nurse to check in with the family. Lucy explained that privacy, security, and nurse availability were nursing values in the ICU.

I swiped my ID badge, the doors swung open, and my senses were immediately assaulted. The air seemed to be actively moving and had an unfamiliar chemical, almost metallic odor. The unit was not exactly noisy, but rather like a beehive hum interrupted irregularly every few seconds with a beep. There were two hallways divided by a nurses' station. It looked like the day shift had two unit clerks chatting with the night clerk. All lights were on in the halls and each room. Nurses moved in and out of the eight private rooms. Everyone seemed to have a purpose and were attending to it. The inside of each room was visible to the hallway giving the impression of a glass wall from the front of the unit to the back. The whole atmosphere seemed important. I looked around and saw Amanda standing against a wall.

"Hi, what's the scoop?"

"Don't know. The clerks over there didn't know we were coming. They asked what I was doing here 15 minutes early if I didn't have anything to do until report."

"Wonder what the best answer is to that crazy question. We are early because we are good nurse residents!"

Amanda smiled and said, "They said I could stand here until Lucy or Candy or Jay showed up."

"Who are Candy and Jay?"

"I hope they are people who know what we're supposed to do."

The door swished open, and Lucy came in smiling. "Hi, Kit and Amanda. Glad to see you're a little early. Both your preceptors are working, but Candy will direct your orientation today. She'll make sure you get a schedule and the ICU orientation manual. Just listen to report on all the patients today. After report, Candy will start your formal orientation. You'll follow her. OK? Any questions? Come down to the conference room."

We were dropped off at the conference room and introduced to the day nurses waiting for report. They were chatting and laughing while each outlined what looked like a report sheet.

"Hi, are any of you Candy?"

"No, she hasn't rolled in yet. Jay was floated to Coronary Care, so you'll meet him some other time."

At 7:00 am on the nose, one of the night shift RNs rolled a computer cart into the room and asked, "Ready, ladies?"

"Hold on, Miss Efficiency. I'm not ready yet."

The most beautiful woman I'd ever seen in scrubs seemed to float in the room. She shoved over Amanda's chair and took a place at the table. Everyone in the room stopped talking. It was hard to tell what the looks on their faces meant but suffice it to say they were more looks of resignation than joy and welcome.

The voice that came from the most exquisitely made-up face ever said, "OK, you may begin."

Amanda started to say something, but the night shift nurse started talking. We were both silent for the next 30 minutes.

Report was quick, detailed and I didn't understand even half of it. Phrases and abbreviations such as Triple-A, immunotherapy, wedge pressures, Gram-negative resistance, and a whole lot more swirled around. I did recognize some of it, especially the cardiac rhythms and arterial blood gas results, but I could not have told you what they meant for the patients' progress even if you threatened to push me off the building. Report terminology moved with such speed that I thought of volunteering to jump off the building halfway through. The nurses wrote down information and asked a question every so often. The atmosphere was exceedingly calm, attentive, and ultra-professional. Except for the beautiful nurse. She inspected her manicure and jotted down a word or two.

As soon as the night nurses left, Amanda quickly said, "Hi. I'm Amanda Milton, and I'm the new nurse resident."

I chimed in, "Hi. I'm Kit Wilson, and I'm also a new nurse resident. We're supposed to be with Candy and Jay, but Jay was floated. Are you Candy?"

The group spontaneously groaned and said, "Good luck. Nice to meet you."

The beautiful nurse held up her hand. "Cut the drama, would you two? I don't need all this excitement so early. So, you're Elissa and Kathy. Yes, I'm Candy. Not Candace. If you had looked at my badge, you would have been able to figure it out." She held out her badge with "Candy, RN" on a large red label at the bottom. "Got it?"

We nodded. "I'll show you what we're going to do today when I have a second. First, I need to make a call. Stay here." Candy didn't wait for an answer and left the room.

"Well, Kathy, what do you think?" asked Amanda.

"Elissa, is it? I think I love your sense of humor, and if we stick together, we might make it out of ICU orientation alive."

Amanda and I were so nervous we nearly collapsed in giggles. "Who's going to tell her our real names? Not me."

I rolled my eyes. "Well, if she looks at our name badges, she can tell. See? Kit, RN, and Amanda, RN. It's a red label. Got it?"

"Oh no. We're screwed."

Candy, not Candace, came back after about 15 minutes. She was holding two enormous notebooks. She presented them to Amanda and me with a flourish. "OK, you two, let's get this show on the road." She closed the conference room door and sat across from us.

She yawned and sighed enormously and yet stunningly. "Let's start first with some ground rules."

Amanda and I opened our orientation notebooks, clicked our pens, and looked expectantly at Candy.

"Stop, right there," she said. "This is not a lecture. Write down what you don't think you can remember, but mainly just listen. OK?"

We nodded.

"First, let's go over your schedule for the first week, then your schedule for the next three weeks. After that, you can decide if you want to finish ICU orientation. Trust me; we will help you decide whether you want to finish the second month. One month is no time at all to learn to be an ICU nurse, but we want to see how well you do in a fast-paced environment. If you think you would want to work here after residency, we need to know how quickly you can put multiple pieces of information together and act correctly on behalf of the patient. That's critical thinking. You've heard of that, right?"

We nodded and gulped in near unison.

We learned that our first week would be three 8 hours shifts in the ICU with either Candy or Jay as our mentor. We would be paid for four hours each day to complete online education modules based on ICU nursing care. These are called ABCDE and are the major body systems that are assessed carefully and continuously in the ICU. The initials stand for Airway or Open Passage from Outside Air to Lungs, Breathing or Rate and Quality of Respirations, Circulation or Cardiac and Circulatory status, Disability or Neurological status, and Exposure or Environmental Effects of Illness. Our enormous notebooks contained information that also covered these topics.

I couldn't take my eyes off Candy. Her skin was nearly perfect, the color of Gram's Christmas toffee. I couldn't tell if she had makeup; the finish was flawless. The top of her head had evenly spaced braids that flowed into a high ponytail secured with a band almost identical to her hair color. Her mouth color and perfect white teeth made her appear like a living, breathing air-brushed photo.

Except that air-brushed photos don't talk and tap perfectly manicured short, rounded pink nails. I must have looked like I was gawking or stunned because the next thing I heard was a long pause and then, "Are you with us, nurse? Do you want to tell me what ABCDE is?"

"Yes," I cleared my throat and put on my attentive face. Thanking heaven above for my advanced medical surgical nursing professor, I could recall the acronym without error.

"Well. That's correct. Thought we lost you in the details. Let's go on," said cunning Candy. "What types of patients are admitted to the ICU?"

We were told that only unstable, critically ill patients were admitted to the ICU. The goal of nursing care in the ICU was to help patients achieve stable physical status so that they could be transferred to a lower level of care, such as 3 North. The best way to think about nursing care in the ICU is to *Stabilize* an Unstable Patient, Achieve a *Trend* of Stability, including pain management and *Transfer* out of ICU. Only patients with unstable and critical status in the ABCDE systems and who are not terminally ill are admitted to the ICU.

Candy acknowledged, "Listen, an eight-hour shift can be tiring, especially when a nurse is new. It may be that you won't have enough energy to complete the required 12 hours of online education on the days that you work in ICU. You do have access to TMH online education when you're at home, right? OK. The point is that we will know when you're online when you've finished each of the five modules and what score you achieved on the competency exam at the end of each module. If you don't get a good enough score on the competency exam, you can review the module again and retake the test until you pass. You can't advance to week two orientation until you pass all five modules, OK?"

Amanda and I must have looked supremely terrified because Candy relented a little bit. "Look, you guys, a lot of this stuff you learned in school. Some of it is new, but it builds on the basics. I want you to either stay here today at one of the open computers in the lab or go home and complete at least one or two of the modules. So, do the Airway and Breathing modules today, OK? We will talk tomorrow. Then, if either you or I think you are in way over your head, we will figure out what to do."

"OK," I said as confidently as I could. Amanda nodded.

It was then 10:00 am and time for break. Candy left us in the room and said, "Break is 20 minutes. Use the facilities, get a cup of coffee and donut, do whatever you want, and be back here at 10:20. OK?"

Amanda looked at me and said, "Break? What's a Break? I haven't had a Break since I started on 3 South!"

"I know! Let's get out of here and go to the lav and the coffee shop before she changes her mind. OK?"

"OK!"

As I mentioned earlier, we were good nurse residents, and we were back in our seats at 10:18 am. Candy returned at 10:25 am. She stood, looking down at us, and said, "Kit? Amanda? Are those your names? Why the devil didn't you say so? Here's a tip. Correct me if I'm wrong, OK?"

"Of course," Amanda said. The look on her face mirrored what I was thinking. No way in blue blazes will we ever correct you!

We toured the ICU next and were able to look at an empty room that was being saved for a later post-operative admission from surgery. Candy reviewed the different sections of the monitoring system, such as cardiac rhythm, respiratory rate, blood pressure reading and trends, pulse oximetry readings and trends, and specialized volume measurements. We then reviewed the various drawers in the Crash Cart. Candy gave us a pretty easy quiz on the purpose of each of the resuscitation medications in the cart. We were both well prepared, which seemed to please her.

Candy introduced us to a patient who was scheduled to be transferred from the ICU to 3 North. Mr. Jeff Conley had had a coronary artery bypass graft or CABG surgery the day before. He was alert and proud to report that he had been up and walked a short distance that morning. Candy asked us what we would think Mr. Conley would want to know before transfer. Amanda said, "That's hard to say since all patients are individual and unique." I nodded sagely. That was the correct answer. I'd heard it a thousand times in school. Candy smiled and assured Mr. Conley that nurses would carefully monitor him on 3 North. She thanked him for taking his time to help in our ICU nurse residency program.

We quietly walked back to the conference room, and Candy shut the door. Then, she turned on us. "Where did you get the idea that patients are so unique and individualized that you can't predict what might be needed? That is such a misunderstanding! What did you think they meant by that in nursing school?

"If every patient was fully unique, how do you think we would be able to do anything at all? If we had to start over with every patient's completely individualized health status, we wouldn't know how to interpret assessment findings or create nursing interventions. Do you think surgeons go into an operating room thinking, "I wonder what I'll find in there when I make the incision?"

The absurdity of what Candy said caused us to break down in laughter. "You know, you two," she said, taking on a more solemn expression, "It is so much better to recognize that people have some basic needs and tolerate limits to their environments in ways that are very often predictable. As nurses, we must appreciate that every person deserves respect and competent care. It's true that people interpret and react in ways that are unique to them, but those ways are not so unpredictable that we can't learn and develop approaches to help."

She paused, and then her face took on a Eureka look. "I've got it! Here's an example. People and cars have some similarities. Every vehicle has some standard equipment. And. All cars perform the same function: to get you from here to there. They all need a fuel source, regular maintenance, and preventive upkeep. Then, there are brands of cars, which are different. Then there are the customized accessories. Every car has its little quirks. But, even so, car owners use standardized information in the owner's manual to understand how to deal with their custom-built and quirky cars.

Candy went on, "Now stop thinking about the sports car you want and work with me here. In residency, you will need to learn the basics, the standard equipment, of critical care. You will find some differences in approaches to patients based on your assessments and evaluation of history and current status. But your job as a nurse will be to make sure that the person's functions and environmental tolerance are evaluated and supported. You are going to learn a little about customizing your skills. Still, most of your time will not be thinking that your patients are so individualized that a useful nursing plan of care isn't possible without some sort of hocus pocus. Get it?"

Amanda and I both nodded. However, I will admit that I didn't quite get it at all. I thought about what Candy said for quite a while afterward until it started to sink in. Her points were complex, rational, and worth considering for all their superficial silliness.

Astoundingly, after comparing nursing to auto mechanics, Candy rewarded us with a real lunch break! A nurse could get whiplash trying to keep up with her. Lunch was supposed to be 30 minutes, but Candy told us to take 45 minutes. We had both brought lunches but decided that in celebration of the first time we had had lunchtime without a patient assignment, we would go to the cafeteria. We splurged on the salad bar.

At 12:45 pm, we were back in our seats. There was no sign of Candy, so we decided to open the enormous notebooks and get a head start on ABCDE. We needed to get a firm handle on the standard equipment before customizing our ICU care!

The afternoon didn't begin until 1:15 pm. Candy seemed happy to see us back again. Although no less gorgeous and put together, she seemed much more approachable in the afternoon. The afternoon's take-home message was You Can't Control What Happens in ICU. What you can control are two things: Your Mindset and Time Management. Candy assured us that we would learn how to use the monitors and that technical skills were simple enough to master. The sense of openness to learning, willingness to think ahead, and staying positive would make us successful as new ICU nurses.

By 2:30 pm, Candy closed her orientation book and said, "Look, you guys, I know this is a whole lot of information for one day. All of us nurses here know that today is just the beginning of a whole lot of information for you. We know that you won't be able to see the obstacles in your path for a whole lot of things. That's why you have a mentor. We also know that time management is probably the hardest skill for new nurses to learn no matter where they work. We get it. We've been right where you are."

"We're here to help you. However, we are here first for the patients. So, to make sure you learn what you need to learn, we will not spoon-feed you information or make it easy because your feelings might get hurt. You have to keep thinking all shift long. Here is a tip. Don't fall into the trap of thinking you are 'overwhelmed' and can't do what we ask you to do. Yes. You can. Stay positive even if you have to pretend for a while. Finish the modules this week and other learning experiences we will give you throughout the next month. Ask questions. OK?"

For the first time that day, we both smiled at Candy.

"Now, you've got another hour before your eight hours are up for today. Go to the skill lab, find a computer, and get started on the modules. Got it?"

"Got it," I said.

"OK," said Amanda.

We gathered up our notebooks, which seemed less enormous and more like lifelines, and walked out.

"Well, I was ready to chuck nursing down the nearest drain this morning when Candy first started in on us. Now, I feel like I want to study and manage my time," said Amanda.

"You said it right, sister," I said. "Talk about a complete personality turnaround from feeling like we were a pain in her neck to feeling like she's in this with us. Let's go figure this out. To the computers!"

Chapter Twenty Three

Re-evaluation Ruminations

ICU orientation started weirdly. Candy seemed disconnected, bored, and even a little annoyed at the beginning of the day. By the end of the day, I had the impression that she would like us to succeed but that we had to be prepared too. I don't care what you say; the car-to-person comparison came out of left field. Time management came up again. I'm determined to figure out how to get things done and still have time to document and think. I'm glad she mentioned attitude or mindset. Hopefully, I can be less frustrated with only one patient to take care of. I've finished one module and will definitely finish the second module before tomorrow morning. The modules are like school, so I didn't have trouble with the first one. The test was simple enough too. Maybe I'll find out that ICU is my passion. It has to be less stressful than 3 North with so many patients every shift. I need to find out what skin care products Candy uses.

I was so confused by Candy's attitude toward Amanda and me initially and couldn't figure out what I had done wrong and why she got so lovely at the end of the day. So, I went to my experts: Gram, Dad, Erin, and Mary. Here is what they said.

Gram: Kit, honey, the world is full of nurses like Candy. Probably not as beautiful but equally puzzling in how they act toward new nurses. In my experience, it often means that she is a little unsure of herself and acts arrogant so that you won't see her own anxiety. Sometimes it means that she is very proud of her own skills because she worked hard to become adept. She wants you to be good too and won't let you just slide by. It could also be that she had something else on her mind this morning, and it has nothing to do with you and Amanda and your orientation. Here's what I think: #1 This is not all about you. #2 Learn what you can from Candy. She has something to teach you. You don't have to be her best friend, but you may have to ask questions carefully. If she's feeling unsure of herself, then a question might threaten her. Don't let your feelings get in the way. Learn from her. #3. The car analogy was undoubtedly creative. Not entirely wrong, but just maybe a bit of a stretch in comparing it to nursing. That's because it leaves out the part of professional nursing that separates us from technicians. I think there was some merit to her point about learning the basic standards of human health status and technical nursing care before you try to go custom. #4. Technical skills are literally primary lifesavers in critical care nursing. You'll need to become competent, or all the compassion in the world won't help your patient. #5. Also, my Kit, don't role-model her behavior and act like a sarcastic rogue. It's not attractive. #6. Did I mention you should learn from her?

Dad: There are lots of nurses and physicians and pharmacists like Candy. Who knows why? They are a pain in my rear when they come into my store with pharmacy interns. I don't think they mean to be so offensive. They're trying to prove something. Ignore her attitude. Learn from her. One thing is for sure. She knows a lot more than you do. Not sure she's a car expert.

Erin: Oh my gosh! There was a prima donna just like Candy in my ICU orientation. It turns out she just liked to hear her voice and get us all scared. It worked. I was afraid, but my mentor was lovely, and I didn't have to work very much with Ms. I Am A Fabulous ICU Nurse. Oh. And my Candy wasn't beautiful. I wanted to give her the name of the guy who cuts my hair. Don't know what kind of car she drives.

Mary: Poor you. I didn't have anyone like that in my residency. You are one incredible lady, though, so I'm sure she was impressed by you. Let me be the devil's advocate here: You know that sometimes I act like a know-it-all when I'm scared, right? Maybe she wasn't that sure of herself and was worried you'd think she wasn't a good mentor. Let me know if you can find out what she uses not to look like she's sweating. I come into work looking perfectly put together, and by the time I run around for an hour or so, I look like a crazed-out nut job. PS I think I had the Rolls Royce of a patient the other day. He made sure we recognized his uniqueness and importance!

So. That was the advice I got. I will probably not ask Candy for her skin care products but will learn from her as much as possible without feeling hurt. I do not like it that almost nothing is all about me anymore. Just saying.

Chapter Twenty Four

"But, when you put your hand to the plough, don't look back."
Florence Nightingale

I honestly looked forward to week two of ICU residency. I had passed all the online modules with flying colors. The technical skills they described were unfamiliar, but the nurses who demonstrated them made them look easy enough. Calculating IV medication drips was intimidating, but we were absolutely assured we would never adjust such crucial medications alone. Jay was my mentor for week two, and Candy was with Amanda.

On my first day of patient care, I had only one patient. She was a woman admitted from the ED at shift change the night before. Her name was Sarah Hunsberger. Looking back on the whole situation, maybe I should have seen some of the issues coming. But I didn't.

The night nurse started report with, "Sorry to leave you guys with the screwed up situation in Bed 2. She shouldn't even be here. Anyway, Sarah Hunsberger is an 86 year old female admitted last evening after being found unconscious at home. Her daughter says she prefers to be called Sadie. Paramedics decided to intubate her, although it doesn't sound like she had any respiratory distress. She's in with possible sepsis secondary to a UTI probably, and possible head injury secondary to a fall or maybe CVA. We cathed her and sent her urine for culture. It looked cloudy and sure looked and smelled infected. Sadie's slowly responsive to voice but doesn't follow commands. No facial drooping. Glasgow score is 10. She opens her eyes to voice command, is saying words occasionally, but I'm not sure what she's trying to say, and she flexes her arms up to painful stimuli. Lower extremities are flaccid. She's due for an MRI of the brain this morning. Urine output has been sufficient every hour and still looks cloudy and dark amber. IV is running well. It's peripheral. She's on the sepsis antibiotic protocol. I didn't have time to do a complete inspection of her skin, so I'll leave that to you. Someone in ED who must have been smoking his socks put in an arterial line, and it could probably come out. Her blood pressures have been stable both arterial and cuff, 110-123/72-84. She's breathing on room air, is still intubated, and hasn't needed respiratory assistance. She's in sinus rhythm, with no arrhythmia. Lungs are clear; she's in no apparent pain. Her daughter has been here all night. Talking to her has given us extraordinarily little to go on. She doesn't know anything about her mother's medical history, meds, or how she's been feeling for the last week or so. She said her mom went to church on Sunday and went out to breakfast with some friends after that. Sarah, Sadie, lives independently, and her daughter thinks she has been caring for all her own needs until this happened. I couldn't get any answers about durable power of attorney, medications, or who her PCP is. According to TIMES, Sadie has been a patient at TMH in the past. We do have the name of her primary physician at that time, but I'm not sure if it's current. Like I said, good luck.

After report, Jay and I walked to Room 2, and he said, "So what do we do first?"

"I'd like to check her labs and see if the urine culture has come back," I said. "Then, let's see if the daughter has remembered anything new."

"No, no, no, no, no," said my clearly exasperated mentor. "How about this? We go look at Sadie. Do you remember the three goals of ICU nursing that Candy covered last week and was covered *quite comprehensively* in your modules?"

"Stabilize, Trend and Transfer," I said proudly.

"Hurray. What did you learn about the first two in report today?"

Slowly, Jay walked me through my first real-world experience with critical thinking on my feet. Sadie's physical condition and level of consciousness had been stable through the night. Her vital signs, Glasgow Coma Scale scores, lung sounds, and urine output have been stable. We completed a head-to-toe assessment and documented findings. We checked on the MRI and found it was scheduled for 10:00 AM.

Jay was walking me through an approach to Sadie's daughter that might help us gain more information when a booming, acerbic voice came into the room from the direction of the nurses' station.

"Oh, isn't that just grand? Dr. Billy is back from vacation," sighed Jay. "Never mind me, Kit. I'll behave. Dr. William Hyde is our medical director. He's been on vacation for the past week or so, and I can tell he's back. It sounds like he's discovered Sadie is a patient here in our ICU. Let's go out and talk to him before he blows a gasket."

"Hi Dr. Hyde," Jay started, "What can I tell you about Mrs. Hunsberger in Bed 2?

"You can start by telling me what a woman who is 86 years old, with a urinary tract infection, is doing in a critical care unit. Don't tell me she might also have a stroke. It doesn't seem like whatever is causing her level of consciousness issues has caused any major system instability. Since when is a perfectly stable geriatric patient considered a reasonable ICU admission? Let's get her extubated, the arterial line out, and transfer her to the floor. Anything about those orders you don't understand, nurse?"

"No, doctor, that is all completely clear. Let me start that transfer process and, in the meantime, see if we can get her family to get us some more data for the 3 North staff."

Dr. Hyde rolled his eyes and said, "Thanks, Jay, I'll get off my high horse now." He looked at me up and down, shrugged, and turned his back on both of us.

"No prob, my new nurse resident and I will get right on that. Come on, Kit."

Now, I thought this might be the easiest first day in ICU in the history of nurse residencies. I was so wrong.

Jay suggested that since it was almost 30 minutes before the first scheduled visiting hours, we complete and document another assessment to assure ourselves that she was still trending as stable. Jay paged the Respiratory Therapy Department to extubate Sadie. I was thrilled when Jay told me I would remove the arterial line. The arterial line was inserted in Sadie's right wrist. It was a short catheter that was connected to the monitor and provided more accurate blood pressure readings than a cuff alone. Arterial lines provide vital information for critically ill patients. Sadie's status had been trending as stable long enough to discontinue the line safely.

Jay asked, "What is the first thing we are going to check before we begin to pull out an arterial line?"

I correctly recalled the need to check clotting studies to guard against excessive bleeding. We obtained the correct sterile tray containing the equipment we would need to remove the sutures and the line. I would maintain firm direct pressure for at least five minutes after the line was removed. We talked about the need to maintain sterility, including gloves and gauze. Removing an arterial line requires careful assessment before and after the removal. I checked the peripheral pulses above and below the line so that I would know if there had been any change after removal.

I started to remove the tape on the dressing, and Jay said softly, "Stop right there, Kit. What did you forget? Who did you forget?" I must have looked blank because he went on, "Didn't we talk to Sadie earlier when we were assessing her? Don't you think we ought to tell her what we're going to do?"

I had forgotten to tell Sadie that I was going to remove some tape and one of her pieces of equipment. Even though Sadie wasn't fully conscious, we didn't know if she could hear or feel us touching her, so we needed to tell her what we were doing. This is such basic nursing that I could feel my stomach drop and cheeks flush. Sadie was a person and deserved the respect I would give to any alert patient. I won't bore you with details, but my technical skill was satisfactory, and Jay said he would sign my orientation sheet saying that I had correctly completed this procedure.

Astonishingly, 27 minutes had been taken up with this assessment and line removal procedure. Jay told the unit clerk that Sadie's daughter could be admitted for visiting.

A very tired-looking woman of about 60 years old came quickly walking into the room. "Hi, how's mom? I'm Holly, Sadie's daughter. You do know to call her Sadie, right? Not Sarah? Did she have a stroke? What are you going to do today to wake her up?"

Jay introduced himself and me and gestured to two chairs in the corner of the room. "Please sit down, ma'am. I'd like to explain to you what is going on this morning."

Jay started by asking if we could find out a little more about Sadie's medical history. Holly agreed to go to Sadie's apartment and look for her medications. We found out that Holly was not married, and she was an only child. Sadie had no other living immediate family in the area. Things were going well until Jay asked if Sadie and Holly had ever talked about a Durable Power of Attorney for Health Care or a Living Will.

"What are you saying? Is she dying? I want everything done for her. Just because she's old doesn't mean you can let her die!" Holly jumped up and threw her upper body over Sadie's chest, sobbing, "Don't die, Mama. I'll make sure they don't pull the plug!"

Dr. Billy strode into the room. He was a tall man with a slim build and biceps bulged in his short-sleeve shirt. The pale green shirt and coordinating tie, along with his half-glasses and gray temples, made for an imposing first impression. "Is there a problem in here?"

Jay explained that Holly was Mrs. Hunsberger's daughter and was concerned about her mother. We were just beginning to discuss the care plan with her.

"My mom is not going to be shoved into a corner and left to die, Doctor," Holly said. "I demand to know what you intend to do with her and why you want to see her will and everything!"

"Madam," the doctor chuckled. "This is an intensive care unit. We take care of people at immediate risk of dying or having serious complications. Look at your mother. How old is she? Listen, she'd be better off out on the regular unit. She doesn't belong here."

"How dare you try to hold her age against her. That's ageism, and I'll report you to the hospital administration!" said Holly.

The doctor shrugged and raised his eyebrows at Jay. "I tried," he said, turning on his heels and walking out of the room.

I quietly closed the door to the room, and Jay helped Holly back to the chair. He quickly reassured Holly that no one was trying to tell her that her mother was dying, nor did Sadie have any life-sustaining equipment at this time. That meant there was literally no plug to pull. Her heart was beating with a normal rhythm. She would have her breathing tube pulled after visiting hours because she was breathing well independently. We asked if Sadie had any documents describing her wishes if she got sick. This is what we meant by Durable Power of Attorney and Living Will. We didn't want to see her final will. Dr. Hyde was trying to say that Holly and her mom would be more comfortable on 3 North. He probably could have done a better job explaining things.

"He certainly could have been more compassionate! Although maybe I shouldn't have threatened to have him fired," Holly said, tearing up again. "Is he always such a jerk?"

"You're exhausted, Holly. That's not helping you think as clearly as you'd like, I'm sure," Jay continued, ignoring her last question. "The news is largely positive today. As Dr. Hyde mentioned, your mom will be transferred out of ICU to a regular hospital floor. The nurses on 3 North will explain about future testing and treatment. That means she is in stable physical condition."

"You can visit whenever you'd like on 3 North," I chimed in. "There will not be set visiting hours, and you can even stay the night if you think that's a good idea."

The door opened quietly. A pleasant-looking guy with a reverend's collar walked into the room. He was carrying a chair and sat on the other side of Holly's chair.

"Hi, I'm Chaplain Harrison," he said. "I understand you are Mrs. Hunsberger's daughter. It sounds like you've had quite a night and morning."

Chaplain Harrison Phillips sat next to Holly as she cried and reiterated that she didn't want her mom to die. He asked Holly if they could talk in the conference room after she and Jay finished talking.

She nodded. "Can you tell me about the will they keep asking for?"

"Absolutely," said the chaplain.

Jay explained the transfer to 3 North again, the MRI to be completed about 10:00 am, and if at all possible, how Holly could help us learn more about Sadie's past medical history by bringing in her meds.

In a matter of moments, Chaplain Harrison brought the tension down in the room to a manageable level. He led Holly out of the room, and both Jay and I exhaled.

"First things first," said Jay. "Let's go thank the unit clerk for calling the chaplain and see how we're coming with obtaining a bed on 3 North. As I hope you can see, we depend on each other to help when things get sticky. I can't explain what Dr. Hyde was thinking when he tried to 'help.' He knows that nurses are better educated to listen and explain treatment plans. Generally, doctors excel at explaining medical treatment changes, and nurses reinforce the information."

The rest of the shift went by quickly. We continued to assess and document Sadie's condition. She was extubated and continued to breathe well with an oxygen cannula in her nose. Holly brought in Sadie's medications from home, and we were able to give her an update and her mom's new 3 North room number.

Sadie remained stable, completed an MRI of the brain, and was transferred to 3 North at about 2:00 pm. I was able to give Lydia the transfer report and was pleased when she said, "Thanks, Kit. Good job."

Jay was waiting for me when I returned from 3 North. "We're getting another admission to Room 2 as soon as it is cleaned. Why don't you take a few minutes break, Kit?"

I decided to look up Amanda and see what she was doing. She and Candy were on the other side of the hall. They were turning and positioning their patient. I waited outside the room and waved when I caught her eye.

Candy came out looking as put-together as ever. "What is it, Kit?" Is everything OK with Jay? Amanda is busy with her hourly assessments right now. Maybe you can check in with her some other time."

I noticed Amanda waving a piece of paper at Candy and me. "Got it," Candy said, nodding at Amanda. "Did Jay show you the hourly sheet? No? Ask him. Amanda thinks this is a good time management tool. All new grads have trouble getting their act together. Probably you are too."

Dutifully, I walked back to Jay and found him chatting in the nurses' station with another nurse. "Can you show me the hourly sheet?" I asked.

Jay explained that the hourly sheet was simply a blank piece of printer paper onto which I was to draw six sections: Report/Labs/Vitals/Orders/Assessment/Misc. Under each section, I would write the shift hours from 7:00 until 19:00. I know it sounds crazy, but I thought it was inspired! In school, I took notes during report and made notes to myself during the day. That worked as fine as wine during school. During 3 North residency, though, my papers were too small, and essential information got jumbled up and lost as I wrote on every available space. I was always behind and couldn't be sure I charted everything. I folded the sheet and placed it in my pocket.

I didn't have to wait long to use the hourly sheet on a genuine ICU-appropriate patient. The new patient arrived in that bed less than one hour after Sadie was transferred. Holy Moley.

Mrs. Debra Gill was admitted into ICU from the ED. She was a 58-year-old woman who was driving home last night around 10:00 pm following an evening with her friends. Somehow, she lost control of her car and landed in a ditch. She called her husband. He called the automotive body shop and came to the accident site. The vehicle was towed, and Mrs. Gill and her husband went home. She seemed to have no injuries other than large bruises on both arms sustained when the airbag deployed. The police were not called. She told her husband that her right leg was sore, so she took two Tylenol at home. They planned to file the accident report right after breakfast this morning. She seemed fine through the rest of the evening and went to bed around 1:00 am. Her husband woke, dressed, and made coffee around 8:00 am. When he had finished reading the paper and his wife was still in bed, he went to check. Mrs. Gill was snoring loudly, was hard to arouse, and had slurred speech.

Mr. Gill called 911. Physician notes in the ED revealed a concussion. Her assessment showed her left pupil larger than the right or anisocoria. Speech was slurred but coherent. Other bruises appeared in the night, and X-Rays showed a fractured right femur. It was a mystery how she managed to walk after the accident. Mr. Gill told the ED staff that his wife and her friends often shared a bottle of wine at their dinners. She agreed to a blood alcohol test even though almost 12 hours had elapsed since she was with friends. The results were low, indicating that she was not intoxicated when the blood test was drawn. Mrs. Gill's admitting medical diagnosis was TBI or traumatic brain injury. CT results were inconclusive for contusion; her Glasgow Coma Scale (GCS) score was 11, indicating a moderate head injury. She was at risk for later onset cranial bleeding, including seizures and possible pulmonary embolism. Nursing priorities centered around neurological assessment, pain management, and safety.

I used my newly discovered hourly sheet and found it made a big difference in recording pertinent assessment patterns before I had a chance to document on TIMES. Jay and I had placed an air mattress on the bed before Mrs. Gill arrived. The ED transport team helped us slide her onto it. The ED nurse practitioner and I adjusted the splint straps on the right leg. I became much more proficient in evaluating neurological status using the GCS. Dr. Hyde noted bilateral ruptured tympanic membranes or eardrums, most likely caused by Mrs. Gill's airbag deployment. Snoring had not been documented since the admission to ED. Debra Gill's head and shoulders were elevated about 30 degrees. She was using oxygen by mask set to deliver 35 percent oxygen. Pain assessment showed Mrs. Gill tolerating any discomfort she may have been experiencing. Since she had a head injury, the use of pain medications, especially narcotics, would be used judiciously. It will be important to have accurate GCS scores, and sedation from narcotics can mask problems. Orthopedic surgery was scheduled for early morning. A heparin drip was ordered to prevent blood clotting from her head injury and fracture. Her GCS scores indicated she was awake enough to basically understand what was going on.

I felt so sorry for Mr. Gill. A son was on his way from out of town but wouldn't arrive until tomorrow. Jay allowed me to explain the various pieces of equipment and orient him to visiting hours and other routines of the ICU. Jay and I encouraged him to hold his wife's hand and talk to her quietly. He asked us to call her Deb or Debbie. I whispered to Jay that I thought Mr. Gill should be allowed to stay after visiting hours. He shook his head. Mr. Gill left when the visiting hour lights flickered, signaling it was time to go.

"The biggest problem I have with ICU visitation is that we don't have time to help family members cope with the stress of severe illness," I said. "Since Mrs. Gill, Deb was stable, letting her husband stay longer wouldn't have hurt anything."

"Tell me, when would you start your hourly checks and documentation? Before or after having a conversation with the patient's husband?" asked Jay with an arched brow.

"Well, afterward."

"How long does it take to complete hourly checks, document, check TIMES for new labs and orders?"

"Let's see." I started my head to toe assessment of Deb, and by the time I finished validating the IV's, oxygen mask and oxygen saturation, cardiac and circulatory status, cardiac rhythm pattern, blood pressure, and trends, urine output, checking the accuracy of three IV lines: heparin, fluid replacement and analgesic, and neurological assessment with GCS, 30 minutes had elapsed. Documenting findings, checking for new orders and new lab/X-Ray results, and giving skin care took almost the rest of the hour.

"Kit, we don't have time to babysit families in ICU. Remember Maslow's hierarchy of needs? What is the most important step that has to be completed before people can move on to higher steps?"

"Physiological," I replied.

"What's number two?"

"Safety," I said, reciting something I'd known since high school.

"Right. Socialization and social relationship building are farther up the ladder," said Jay. "We have to make sure the patient's physiology and safety needs are taken care of first. Most of the time, we don't have time to chat with the family except to give them a brief update and answer clarifying questions. In ICU, the physical takes priority. If you think the family is having trouble, call the chaplain or the social worker."

"That doesn't seem very compassionate," I said.

"Well, maybe not in a hand-holding way, but keeping our careful attention on the critically ill body and not the psyche is compassion in an unstable patient, I believe."

Debbie Gill's neuro assessment remained steady, but oxygenation levels began to fluctuate within the next hour. She became restless, and GCS decreased, indicating her level of consciousness was declining. By 6:00 pm, the decision was made to intubate. She was placed on a ventilator and sedated. An arterial line was inserted. Oxygen saturation, arterial blood gases, and cardiac rate all stabilized.

Mr. Gill was allowed to visit briefly. I asked him if he would like to see a chaplain and the alarmed look on his face confirmed I had said something wrong.

"Is she going to be gone soon? Should I tell my son to hurry so he can see her?" he asked.

"Oh no, Deb is responding very well, just as we said. I just wondered if you wanted someone to talk to."

He sadly smiled. "No, that's OK. Just take care of her. I'm fine right now." He kissed Deb's forehead and walked out of the room.

Jay and I had a silent communication moment. His eyebrows went up even further as if to say, "See?" My brows furrowed. "OK, OK. Maslow. Got it."

Chapter Twenty Five

"There is no part of my life upon which I can look back without pain."
Florence Nightingale

I left work feeling like I had been hit on the head with a rock. The amount of emotion that I saw today within patients' families and my own feelings about wanting to care for those families' emotional and the patients' physical needs had me feeling like being on a merry-go-round! Every time I looked up, something different was going past. Hourly assessments, hourly documentation, visiting hours, reporting negative findings, and setting up for intubation and arterial line insertion while constantly looking at my watch so I could be on time for the next thing to come around. Calculating titrated drips like heparin was more complicated than I remembered from school. I was terrified of making a mistake. Jay always double-checked me, and I checked the machine every half hour. The Patient Controlled Analgesia or PCA was set to deliver a baseline dose of non-narcotic pain medication. When she became more alert, Deb would be allowed to self-administer pain medication as needed.

Jay reviewed with me how to monitor analgesia amount and calculate dosage received. There was so much to remember. Jay had to remind me to look at the clotting lab studies. Thank God I got the hourly sheet when I did. What a flippin' mess it would have been without it. I couldn't go right home and face the family. They would want me to talk out my feelings, hug me, tell me I'm the best nurse they know, and feed me whatever I wanted. The last didn't sound too bad since I wanted ice cream. I headed toward our charming one-block Main Street. I love that the stores have striped green awnings in the summer, and every store is owned by someone who lives in town. When I was at TSU, I was teased about coming from Disney Town. "Practically perfect, with apologies to Mary Poppins," I would always respond. Thompson isn't in the dark ages, though. We have big box retail and chain grocery stores too. They are just thoughtfully placed on the edge of town. Anyway, I parked right in front of Jake's Market. Jake's specializes in homemade ice cream and fresh meats. It's a strange combination, but it works.

I don't know how long I stood looking at the list but was shocked from my decision-making stare: Chocolate chunks with strawberry swirl or Chocolate chunks with fudge swirls, or Birthday Cake with vanilla ice cream and white cake mixed with raspberry.

A familiar voice asked, "Have time for ice cream?" It was Susan, my night mentor. She had the night off and came in to get some Jake's outstanding bratwurst.

I believe in karma or coincidence, or whatever you call it, when a person shows up just at the time you need them.

"Hey, don't cry," she laughed. "You look like you need more than one scoop."

Susan got a cone, and I settled for two scoops: one of each chocolate chunk. I poured my heart out to her telling her about my terribly busy, terribly terrible clinical day in ICU.

"It doesn't sound too bad," she said.

"Seriously? I never stopped moving once we got the second patient. And there is never time to talk to families. And I'm sure I forgot to do or document something. And my mentor reviewed Maslow's Hierarchy of Needs to show me that compassion is mainly physiological in the ICU. I'm so tired of people telling me that I don't understand 'caring' because I want to establish a relationship with patients and families. Nursing is surely not the satisfying career I thought it would be. I don't have time to do anything but run around. Susan, I think I might be in the wrong field. That sucks too because I want to move into an apartment, and I need the money."

Susan finished her cone and let me talk. Then, we sat quietly while I plunged into my ice cream. I started to feel better whether from being listened to or having my blood sugar skyrocket; I was not sure.

Then, Susan told me that I wasn't the first nurse to feel like this. Every new nurse thinks they're crazy and ill-prepared. She thought I needed to be around other nurses to get more advice about approaches to compassion and caring. She said, "you know it looks different in real life than in the textbook."

Really? Well, Nurse Susan, I figured that out for myself. Does anybody want to tell me just what that is supposed to mean? I could have a terrible time working in many other places without the hassle and fear of missing something essential and hurting another person. (Can you tell I was royally ticked off?)

"I know you and I have talked about meeting to quilt and talk, but I think I have a better idea than just me. You need a support crowd. I know just the group. I'm hosting S&S next Thursday at my house. It's short for Sip and Stitch. We're a group of 3 North nurses who meet every month to stitch on their projects like quilting, knitting, embroidering, or crocheting. Of course, some of us just Sip because we're not crafty."

The idea was to bring a beverage of your choice: adult beverages and soft beverages were welcome. Whoever is the host also provided a snack. Since Susan was hosting that month, she will make a couple of cheese balls with crackers, olives, and raw veggies. Not too fancy. Perfect. Susan said everyone talks about what's going on in their lives which, of course, includes work. She practically begged me to come and bring my beverage. And I will. My quilt squares, wine cooler, and

I were on board. If I tell my residency story, what's the worst that could happen? The other nurses could confirm I should have majored in something else in college and should run for the nearest hospital exit. Maybe they'll tell me the secret of nursing in real life. Something's got to give, or I'm on the next train out of nursing.

Chapter Twenty-Six

"Nursing is an art and if it is to be made an art, it requires an exclusive devotion as hard a preparation as any painter's or sculptor's work."
Florence Nightingale

The rhythm of ICU had a resolute feel. There was a purposeful cadence to staff movement in the hallways, the choreographed feeling of nurse movements around patients' beds as monitors were evaluated, hearts and lungs were assessed, intake and outputs were totaled, and IV medications were titrated according to the response. Information was key. Knowledge was indeed power in the ICU; lack of knowledge could have devastating results. Data were analyzed and discussed. Nurses, physicians, and technicians seemed to have an open and focused professional persona. Family communication was almost exclusively patient-centered and delivered pleasantly but matter-of-factly. Nursing communication with patients was a fascinating blend of explanation during procedures accompanied by a hand squeeze or arm pat upon entering and before leaving the room. By the end of week two in the ICU, I knew enough to be both awed and intimidated. It was probably the most motivating environment of my young career so far.

I grew to respect Jay more each day. He was, of course, a technical wizard with ICU equipment. His ability to anticipate what was needed next seemed as normal as breathing to him. I felt like the little kid that said, "When I grow up, I want to be just like you." However, the thing about Jay that caught me really off guard was his occasional and unpretentious nonverbal kindness toward patients. I say it that way because although Jay was a firm mentor and didn't allow me to wallow in pity for patients, he showed humanity that I had only read about in books. It is one thing to read about and commit to respecting every patients' human dignity, and it is another thing to see it in action.

Jay made it clear that in the ICU, technical competence and analysis of patient data went hand in hand. Every time we looked at diagnostic test results or performed hourly assessments, he would say, "Knowing what you know about this patient, how is this information important, Kit?" After my answer (which was never complete enough, by the way), he would say, "OK. What are you going to do about this information, Kit?"

He made me think so carefully that I left with a low-grade headache every day. You can take this as a fact: Every day off, I reviewed that giant ICU notebook! One night, I even woke up saying out loud, "Here is what I'm going to do: report the lower potassium level and remember to mention the urine output trend." I was pleased with my answer and fell back asleep.

One more thing about the nurses in the ICU: They seemed to have an amazing filter for the tragic things they saw every day. Also, they were ironically amusing. My psych professor would probably say it's a defense mechanism to think about awful human events in a gentler light. I don't know why, but to this day, the people I know who can best explain life through a lens of opposites and humor are ICU nurses.

Even Candy! The other day, she and Amanda met Jay and me going down the hall in opposite directions. "Don't you just love the attention that TMH pays to our exercise needs? My watch says I walked seven miles today around the unit! So considerate." Maybe you had to be there, but she barely moved her mouth and looked straight ahead with a solemn expression. Hilarious.

This morning our patient was Donna Robinson. She was alert yet medicated for pain. Jay said, "OK, Mrs. Robinson, we're going to turn you on your right side, listen to your lungs, rub lotion on your back and straighten your sheets. OK?" She nodded understanding. We repositioned her, and I checked her GCS score using hand grasps and foot flexion as commands. She was oriented to her name, knew the year and the events that led to her ICU admission.

"Call me Donna, please, it's 2018, I can't read the day of the week on that board without my glasses, and I had a heart attack after surgery, so that's why I'm here instead of at home. Which is where I should be."

"Excellent, Donna," Jay complimented. "Today is Wednesday. Let me ask your husband to bring in your glasses. That's it for now. I see him and your mother waiting to come in for visiting hours."

He turned to leave and then pivoted back. With a thoughtful expression, he said, "I forgot. Donna, now, I'd like you to jump out of bed while reciting the alphabet backward." A grin quickly followed her startled look. "Right away, Nurse," she said, giggling. "As soon as you run and get me that steak dinner I asked for!"

Phil Robinson and Donna's mom gasped behind me and hugged each other. "She's better! Thank God she's better!"

Jay squeezed Donna's hand, nodded at the visitors, and said, "Here are your visitors. Paperwork calls. See you later."

We walked to the nurses' station out of earshot. "Now, Kit, why did I ask Mrs. Robinson to jump out of bed?"

"Um, to be silly?"

"Very insightful. Why would I want to be silly?"

"You thought she might laugh?"

"Again, genius answer. What message, other than being silly, did that comment send?"

I racked my brain. "I don't exactly know."

Jay reviewed Mrs. Robinson's history with me for the next few minutes. She was a 52-year-old woman with a history of Type I diabetes since age 19. She had hypertension that was well controlled with medication. She had been married for 22 years. No children. Her mother was alive, healthy for her age, and lived independently. Donna had felt extreme fatigue and left arm discomfort for about a month. Diagnostic testing showed the need for triple coronary artery bypass graft (CABG). Once in surgery, it was discovered that four bypasses were needed. Donna had an uneventful recovery for the first eight hours after surgery. Then she experienced crushing chest pain. Her monitor began to show extra or ectopic beats, and a 12 lead EKG had changes that appeared to be a heart attack or myocardial infarction (MI). Lab studies confirmed a postoperative MI, which is an uncommon complication. She was transferred to ICU, where appropriate interventions were started. By the time we cared for her two days later, she still had one chest tube. Her kidney function, affected by diabetes, showed inadequacy initially, but urine output had improved, and her electrolytes were back in acceptable limits. She continued using oxygen at 30 percent O2 and had no immediate respiratory distress. She could speak clearly but became tired quickly. Donna was a sick lady but showing improvement.

"Kit, now think. Consider if you had a family member in ICU and they almost died. Then the doctors told you they were improving; what might make you believe it a little?"

"If they looked or acted better."

"Hurray! That's right! Is laughing a normal response to a silly question?"

"Yes." I couldn't believe I was so thick. "You let the family see for themselves that there has been some improvement."

A couple of nurses in the station began to applaud. "Good answer, Good answer!" "You've got a keeper there, Jay!"

I flushed and took a slight bow. "I have so much to learn!" Awkwardness Central. I hate being the center of attention.

To my total embarrassment, I heard Candy behind me. "Don't let them get to you, Kit. You learned about hope today. Jay is a master at instilling appropriate levels of hope."

Amanda was, of course, right next to Candy. "You know what was in the Emotional Reactions to ICU module? Fear of a loved one's death can cause sheer terror in a family. The nurse in the video called it a Soul Injury."

Jay and Candy looked dumbfounded.

"Amazing. You two have earned a lunch off the unit," said Jay.

Candy nodded. "You watched a teaching video after work last night? Astonishing. You can go now, right Jay?"

We left before they changed their minds about Amanda's perceptive insight.

"I'm learning so much," I started.

"Me too. So many awful, depressing things are going on. At least I have a mentor who isn't interested in my feelings about working here. I hate this place."

"You hate ICU? Do you mean you're still not sure about staying in nursing? Some days I think that what I do, or rather what nurses who have a clue do, is important and impressive. Then a couple of minutes later, I begin to think that we just postpone the inevitable and are complicit with the doctors in making more suffering. Then, a patient turns around a little and, like Jay made Donna and her family feel better about the chance of recovering and then…sorry, I'm blabbing," I said, trying to keep up with Amanda. "There's no race to the cafeteria. We get 30 minutes."

We'd reached the cafeteria, and Amanda went to the salad bar frowning and poking at the choices like a judge on a cooking show. I got the hospital's famous green pepper soup, veggies with hummus, and ice water and found a seat in the corner where we could talk.

"You know," Amanda said as she plopped down, "when I was in nursing school, I thought that if I could avoid fainting at the sight of bodily fluids, I could be a nurse. What a naïve conclusion. I still gag at the smell of poop and puke and the smell of the ICU...what is that odor anyway...blood, Gram-negative sepsis, and death with a fine overlay of disinfectant?" she paused to look at a forkful of greens and put them back in the bowl.

"It's not the smells or the blood. It's the suffering and the unfairness of what's happening to these people. That's what I hate and can't do a blessed thing about...I do not belong in nursing. Period. The end."

"Umhmm. Right," I said. Something was bugging me, and I couldn't put my finger on it. I hadn't thought about how the patients felt about the awfulness of their situation. I was concerned with my time management and technical skills, knowledge of their condition, nursing needs, and whether I said the right things. I kept thinking about what I could do to make them feel grateful for my caring and the best ways to avoid making a mistake. There was something off, but I didn't get it.

"I need to pay the rent," Amanda went on. "I'm not like you and live at home for free. No offense. You've made me feel better."

"None taken. Listen. You've helped me too. Could we meet more often and talk about things? I want to have to pay the rent too, and I can't get out of my parents' house until I find something. I can't afford anything if I don't work at a decent salary job. My brother says I want too much for my first apartment. I'm determined to afford Chateau Bordeaux!"

Amanda laughed. "I live in the complex just off the freeway. The Windmill. No windmill in sight. The owners must be Dutch or want to see the Netherlands or something. It's OK. Safe and close to work. But the Chateau Bordeaux! Wow. You are so posh, Kit! Let me know if you figure out how to afford that place on a TMH nurses' salary. I'll move in next to you!"

We returned to ICU. I felt a little braver than when we left.

Chapter Twenty-Seven

**"Rather ten times die in the surf...
than stand idly on the shore."**
Florence Nightingale

The penultimate shift in ICU was my "make and almost break" experience as a nurse resident.

Jay passed me off to another nurse because he thought I'd benefit from the experience. This had happened to Amanda a few times, so I wasn't shocked. Nothing seemed odd as I began the "beneficial experience."

"Kit, I want you to work with Nora Larger today," he said. "She is taking care of Sharon Roth. Nora could use an extra pair of hands, and I think you could learn a lot from her."

"C'mon," Nora said. "Let's get going. I know you heard in report, but let's just review because there's a lot here. Sharon is a 34 year old female admitted last evening following what seemed to be a fainting episode with jerky motions at home. She had a day-long headache and lower abdominal pain. Sharon is under treatment from her primary physician for an E.Coli urinary tract infection. When she got to Emergency last evening, her white blood cells were elevated at around 32,000 with a left shift. Her fever was 102.2 degrees Fahrenheit or 39 degrees Celsius. She had a foley catheter inserted, and hourly urine outputs ran from 20-23 milliliters. Her pulse ox was 90 on admission but has been 96-98 with a mask at 40 percent oxygen. Blood pressures have been running 80 systolic on admission, now 90-100 systolic and

50-58 diastolic; fluids are keeping the BP stable, plus she has a titrated dopamine drip at five micrograms/kg/minute. She's in sinus rhythm at 85-89 beats per minute. She's in Gram-negative septic shock. We're waiting for the clotting studies to return, but platelets are low at 100,000."

To translate, Sharon was one sick cookie. Here's a general lay person's version, so you get a picture of Sharon's health state. She had probably had a seizure following a headache from an unknown cause and lower abdominal pain likely from her urinary tract infection. The bacteria causing her infection was in a category called Gram-negative. This is not a specific name of a bacteria, but Gram-negative bacteria often cause more severe disease than Gram-positive bacteria. I knew this meant Sharon's sepsis, which is a body-wide infection, would probably require a complex antibiotic treatment plan. Sharon's white blood cells were elevated much higher than the 10,000 normal high limit. She had a severe infection. The "left shift" meant that bacteria probably caused her infection. Her kidneys were not producing urine in adequate amounts. The least acceptable amount of urine made every hour is 30 milliliters. Her kidneys may have been shutting down. Kidneys are organs necessary for life, so this sign was also a huge source of concern. Her oxygen levels were low on admission, but she responded adequately (but not wonderfully) with a pretty high oxygen level by mask. Her platelets were low, and since platelets are needed for blood clotting, Sharon was at risk for bleeding. Her blood pressure was abnormally low on admission, and she's receiving a medication, dopamine, which will strengthen her heart, increase blood flow to her kidneys and cause her blood vessels to constrict, raising her blood pressure. The dopamine dose may need to be adjusted every hour or more often to keep her blood pressure at a level that will give enough blood to her lungs, brain, and other vital organs. Her heart rate and rhythm were about the only pieces of assessment data that were normal. Are you intimidated yet? Not for the first time, I wondered what in the world I was doing in an ICU caring for someone that sick.

Nora was one of the most skilled and most congenial nurses in the ICU. She took the time to explain what Sharon's condition meant for our nursing care and outlined our work for the day. Most of the day was a disciplined mix of assessment, analysis of changes, communication with the medical team, and adjustments as needed. Dr. "Billy" Hyde was on duty today with Dr. Elliott Barre as his backup in the coronary care unit. Assessments were completed every hour. If Sharon had a medication change, then assessment occurred immediately, every 15 minutes twice, and every 30 minutes twice before returning to hourly checks. We monitored Sharon's vital signs, cardiac rhythm, neurological and cardiac respiratory status. Sharon's hourly urine output steadily increased during the morning and was at the magic number of 30 milliliters by 10:00 AM. We adjusted medications to support her low blood pressure and kept an extra IV infusing for multiple antibiotics and fluid replacement. I assisted with an arterial line insertion to monitor Sharon's exact blood pressure and provide a port to draw arterial blood gases and very frequent lab studies. The lab studies we particularly paid attention to were hemoglobin level, platelet count, clotting studies, and antibiotic peak and trough levels. Sharon's clotting studies were borderline abnormal, and her hemoglobin level was low. Her blood was typed and cross-matched in case transfusions were needed. I applied continuous pressure for five minutes after laboratory studies were done and when the arterial line was inserted. She did not have excessive bleeding from those sites.

Sharon was awake but drowsy, and Nora told her everything we were doing before we did it. If there would be a sensation associated with a procedure or request, such as coughing and deep breathing or skin care, Nora explained what Sharon should expect.

We wore a gown and gloves to prevent contamination. IV ports were wiped with alcohol before giving antibiotics or performing blood draws. I changed my gloves every time a pair was contaminated, such as between IV access and physical care. My eyes scanned every piece of equipment, and I was hyperaware of drawing conclusions about each monitor reading and what those conclusions meant for Sharon's clinical state. I was absorbing Nora's directions and explanations like a sponge.

Sharon's husband, Mark, visited at the appointed time and was updated on her condition. Dr. Hyde came into the room. "She's not out of the woods yet, but I think we've got the right antibiotics for the infection in her blood. We know she's showing improvement because her blood pressure and urine output are stabilizing. We're especially watching her blood clotting studies," he said. "Any questions?" he asked, walking out of the room.

Mark nodded and held Sharon's hand. "I'm right outside, babe," he said. "Your mom's flying in later today. The doctor says you're doing better. Keep it up."

He turned to Nora and me. "Thank you for all you're doing. We're not from around here. My brother is driving up from San Davers after he gets off work, and Sharon's mom is coming from the West Coast later this afternoon. You nurses are so wonderful."

Nora smiled and touched his arm. "You're welcome, Mark. I'm sure you'll be glad when you have someone to wait with. Ask about anything you don't understand, OK?"

He teared up and shook his head. "I'll be outside. Just take care of my Sharon. She's my life."

I wanted to wrap my arms around Mark Roth and tell him everything would be alright that Sharon would be OK. The look on my face must have alerted Nora. She motioned me out to the hall.

"You know, it's understandable to want to offer reassurance because Mark is so scared. Remember when he thanked us? He wants to be sure we know his wife is important and to like her enough to take care of her."

"Like her enough?" I asked. "What do you mean? Does he think if we don't like her, we won't give her our best?"

"I know that sounds like superstitious thinking, but yes, that's right. Mark doesn't know us yet, and a part of him wants to butter us up a little. That doesn't mean he isn't truly grateful. He's only doing what he thinks will help ensure she gets the best care. Dr. Hyde's time to explain and listen helps him believe that we understand his fear and empathize with him. The way we approach him with an openness to his concerns has let him know that we are sensitive to his need for hope and information."

"How do you keep it together when family members like Mark are so worried? Why don't you feel like crying too?" I asked.

"Of course, I feel his anxiety," Nora said. "That's what empathy is, you know. Somebody told me once it's 'your pain in my heart.' Even though our main focus is life support in critical care, a good nurse leaves family members with the sense that we realize and respect their love and concern. That doesn't mean that I feel like he does. It means that I let him know we appreciate his love and worry."

"Your pain in my heart," I repeated. "That's so right. So right!" I remembered Gram's advice to stay in my own shoes while conveying concern. Empathy is a shared human response. It felt like a bit of light was visible at the back of a heavy curtain.

"You know, most families don't remember all our names, but they do remember when they feel understood. That's good enough," said Nora. "Now, let's concentrate on our next set of assessments and documentation. We put on our game faces and went back to our rhythmic assessments. We have work to do with Sharon. Let's get back in the room, begin with the neuro exam, and work our way down."

"I'm glad that's over," said Sharon. "Mark is such a worrier. I think visiting made my headache come back. Is there anything

I can take for it?" The blood pressure cuff began to expand automatically. The reading on the NIBP unit was 96/58 with a pulse oximetry reading of 96. Her urine output was 32 millimeters, and the color was now pink instead of amber yellow. The cardiac monitor showed a sinus tachycardia of 110, faster than the previous hour by about ten beats/minute.

Nora noted the assessment data and said, "I'm going out to the desk for a second. I'll be right back. Please continue the neuro exam and get another blood pressure, Kit."

I completed the GCS and asked, "Sharon, tell me about your vision. Can you see me clearly?"

Sharon opened her eyes. "Everything is kind of blurry. I just don't feel good, like really funny, and my stomach hurts down here." Sharon rubbed her lower abdomen and closed her eyes.

I noticed the most recent blood pressure was 98/54 with a pulse of 112 and pulse ox of 95.

Sharon opened her eyes and stared blankly at me. Then her eyes rolled back, and she began to shake in every part of her body. I recognized that Sharon was having a grand mal or full tonic-clonic seizure. Trying to keep from running out of the room screaming, I called out, "I need help in Room 3 STAT." I should have pressed the emergency button on my phone or the wall, but I was shocked and forgot. Loud calling out is frowned on in hospitals. It is frightening to other people, especially visitors and patients. Shouting can cause a delay in response due to panic. Emergencies are to be handled quietly and immediately.

I put down the head of the bed and rolled Sharon on her left side to keep her airway open, making sure the oxygen mask stayed in place and that all the IV and arterial line tubes were accounted for and not pulling.

Nora practically flew into the room with an IV bag and tubing with Dr. Hyde on her heels. She began a bolus of medication to stop the seizure. At the same time, she asked another nurse to have Anesthesia paged STAT.

"Tell me what happened, Kit," she asked as the room soon filled with nursing and medical assistance.

"Seizure began at 10:36 and 30 seconds," I remember saying.

Someone pulled in the crash cart and opened it. A nurse anesthetist rushed in and went to the head of the bed, nodding to Dr. Hyde, who ordered oral intubation for ventilation support. Sharon was now unconscious and barely breathing. Her heart rate was in the 40s. I helped position her on her back. The endotracheal tube was inserted and secured. Oxygen was delivered directly through the tube, and the nurse anesthetist verified that breath sounds could be heard in both lungs. Sharon coughed, and I heard, "Bright red mucous from ET tube, doctor."

Sharon's seizure slowed and stopped after two minutes and 15 seconds. I called out this information but could see her condition was rapidly deteriorating.

"New lab results," called the unit clerk.

Nora took them in one smooth move, looked at the results, and handed them to Dr. Hyde. Sharon's calcium was low. Her platelets were lower than two hours ago, prothrombin time and D-Dimer were both elevated.

"Not to state the obvious gang, but what we are dealing with here is DIC," said Dr. Hyde in an almost supernaturally calm voice. "Call blood bank and get those platelets and fresh frozen plasma."

Sharon's lab tests showed she had developed a rare, life-threatening complication of sepsis. Her blood had begun clotting abnormally in small and medium-sized blood vessels. Those clots obstructed her vital organs, such as kidneys, lungs, and brain. This abnormal clotting used up all the blood factors that Sharon needed to clot normally. She then began to bleed, to hemorrhage. This condition is called DIC or disseminated intravascular coagulation. DIC is a life-threatening condition. DIC can occur quickly or slowly. Sharon's DIC progressed at supersonic speed.

I was terrified. Ten minutes after I called for help, the team worked to save Sharon's life with focused coordination.

I became aware that the room was silent except for Dr. Hyde's voice, "I want those platelets. Now. Get a unit of whole blood too. Both IVs were opened wide,

Nora said, "I am beginning CPR."

There were blood-soaked sponges in the bed and on the floor. Dr. Hyde's arms were tightly crossed.

The critical care intensivist from Coronary Care, Dr. Barre entered the room. "I'm here, Bill," he said. "I've called for any available surgeon."

A surgeon quickly walked into the room. He was in surgical garb but didn't stop to scrub or put on a gown. He opened and donned sterile gloves. A unit of blood was hanging on an IV pole and running into Sharon's IV. The anesthetist had started a third IV. The cardiac monitor began beeping irregularly.

"Where is this lady's family?" someone asks.

"I've asked for Chaplain Harrison Phillips to be called," I said from the corner of the room.

"I'm here," said the chaplain. "Mr. Roth is in a private conference room. His brother is with him."

"As you can see, we are in the middle of an unholy situation, Reverend," said Dr. Barre. "No offense intended. Could you keep him company while we sort this out? It will be best if you let him know his wife has developed a complication, and we will be out soon to talk with him."

"Done," said Chaplain Harrison and left the room.

For the next three hours, the team worked with Sharon. Her bleeding seemed to slow after the platelets were infused. Her blood pressure stabilized with a dopamine increase, but her urine output remained low. Blood products continued to be infused, and blood work was drawn after to see if Sharon was responding. The blood work continued to indicate Sharon remained in DIC. The code team moved on after about an hour. Dr. Hyde gave Mark an update. His brother had arrived, and both visited briefly. They both seemed appropriately worried, and Mark looked like a wide-eyed ghost. They were waiting in a private conference room. Lucy told us that she watched them and had provided coffee and snacks. We should just concentrate on Sharon.

At 1:17 pm, Sharon began to bleed from her nose. Dr. Hyde came in a moment after Nora pushed her call button. This time, we managed without the whole team. I attached pressure bags to push blood products and took notes on my report sheet. Urine output was now obviously red-streaked. Dr. Hyde called the surgeon again. Sharon's abdomen was becoming firmer with each 10-minute assessment. There was nothing surgical that would help. Sharon's heart rate slowed, and the respiratory therapist manually ventilated her lungs through the ET tube. Dr. Barre came and consulted with Dr. Hyde. CPR began. The room was almost humming with expert (and me) critical care staff assessing and treating Sharon's rapidly deteriorating condition. Chaplain Harrison was paged again. Lucy came and went without saying a word. I thanked God Lucy, who understood what was going on was with Mark.

By 3:00 pm, it was all over. Dr. Hyde's order stopped CPR. Sharon had died from uncontrolled DIC bleeding. Dr. Barre pronounced the time of Sharon's death. The team left. Lucy quietly told us she would stay with Mark and his brother while Dr. Hyde talked to them. Dr. Hyde looked visibly shaken and upset. Nora and I were left to clean up Sharon and the room.

As he was leaving, Dr. Hyde tapped Nora on the shoulder. Turning his back to me, he said, "Nora, I don't know what this new nurse did, but don't ever leave such an incompetent newbie alone with a patient this sick. God only knows what could have been prevented."

"Dr. Hyde, I was with Kit all morning. You and I saw the labs after the seizure started. Kit called us in here moments after the seizure began. She was not left unsupervised and did nothing wrong," Nora said.

"Listen, I call 'em like I see 'em," he said. "This is why we don't hire new nurses in ICU."

With that, he and Dr. Barre walked out, saying to one another, "We did everything possible. With that much blood loss ..." their voices trailed off as they walked away toward the horrible task of talking to Mark.

I just met her today, I thought, and now she is gone. I didn't know her. She was so scared and yet so brave. Sharon is the first patient who died while I cared for them. I stood looking at Sharon's still body when I heard Dr. Hyde quasi-reprimanding Nora about me. My heart skipped a beat.

"Excuse me," I said, leaving right behind the physicians. "I'll be right back." I got to the nurses' restroom just in time before the sobs broke. I cried and cried until I threw up. Then I deep breathed until I had hiccups. How much of this was my fault? What happened that I should have seen? I splashed water on my face and silently thanked the person who put mouthwash in the restroom.

Nora was picking up the packaging from the floor. The mop and bucket were outside to clean up the bloody floor. Someone had shut the room door, and all the glass door blinds were down, I started talking right away.

"How could she die? I know what happened, but that's so unfair! What's going to happen to her husband? And Sharon's mother lost her child. It's a horrible tragedy, and no explanation is good enough. How did she get so sick so fast? She was seconds from medical care when she had her seizure. How could she die from a urinary tract infection? What did we do wrong?"

"Kit, you did nothing wrong. We'll talk when we're finished. Please. Concentrate on getting Sharon's body ready for her husband," said Nora.

As we worked, Jay came in to help. We carefully cleaned up Sharon, placing a clean gown on her. We cleaned the room of blood, sponges, and other surgical drapes and instruments. We placed clean sheets on Sharon's bed. I brushed Sharon's hair while Nora cleaned her face and body and applied a fine layer of lotion. Jay brought us a warmed blanket so that she wouldn't feel cold to the touch.

"It's OK," Jay said. "The first one is the hardest, and this was a zinger." I nodded, hoping my poor excuse for a game face wasn't too blotchy.

"Mark Roth is ready when you are. His brother and the chaplain are with him," Lucy said.

"Helping Sharon's husband through this part is difficult and very important," said Nora. "Just come along with me, Kit. I'll talk."

Chapter Twenty-Eight

<u>"We must not talk to them or at them but with them."</u>
<u>Florence Nightingale</u>

L ucy looked up when we walked into the conference room. "If you would like to see and spend some time with Sharon, they are ready for you now."

Nora sat briefly in front of Mark and took his hands. "I'm so sorry for your loss," she started. "I want to let you know what to expect when you go into Sharon's room now."

Mark just stared with red-rimmed eyes as Nora explained that all the tubes and monitors had been removed. Mark and his brother wouldn't be left alone but could stay as long as they'd like. She paused and let the information sink in.

Taking Mark's arm, Nora led the way, followed by Lucy holding Mark's brother's arm and Chaplain Harrison to room 3. I brought up the rear.

Dr. Hyde was in the room. He had changed into clean scrubs without blood stains and looked unsettled. He shook Mark's hand and stood across from him.

The clean room and Sharon gave off an eerily quiet vibe. Sharon was in the center of the room, covered to her neck with a blanket, on a stretcher.

Mark just stared at Sharon for a long few minutes. He touched the blanket and her face and said he thought she looked peaceful, like she was sleeping. He hoped she didn't suffer.

"No," said Dr. Hyde.

Chaplain Harrison stayed near the door. He said nothing but felt to me like a support presence.

We all stood by the stretcher. Mark couldn't take his eyes off his wife. "I need to sit down."

I looked at Mark and noticed all the color had drained from his face. Nora had a chair pulled up. She helped him sit down. "Mark. Are you OK?" she said as she wiped away a tear.

He nodded. As he sat back in the chair, the color started to return to his face.

We sat together with Sharon. Words weren't necessary, just presence. Mark slowly stood, using the side rail for support.

Nora gently asked Mark which funeral home he would want and assured him that the funeral home would come for Sharon. Mark could call the funeral home tomorrow to make further arrangements.

"I'm going to go now. I have phone calls to make and a plane to meet. Sharon's mom is in the air and is due to arrive soon. Don't worry. I have a ride," he said, touching his brother's hand across the bed.

We walked him to the door, and he turned and hugged Nora with a sob. "Thank you for crying," he said. "It means a lot."

Chapter Twenty-Nine

"This is not individual work. A real nurse sinks self."
Florence Nightingale

Nora turned to me as the two men walked out of the ICU. "I know this seems harsh, but the best thing for us is to take a quick break and get back to work today. It's never easy to lose a patient, but something this dramatic and visual in a young person is especially hard. We can talk again tomorrow."

Toward the end of the shift, Chaplain Harrison returned and briefly talked with Nora and me in the conference room. I reiterated my memories.

"This is not the only time we will talk, Kit," he said. "Think of this time as first aid for a severe wound. I'll come back tomorrow, and we can talk longer."

We went to the locker room and changed from bloody scrubs into hospital issue clean scrubs. I put my soiled scrubs in a patient belonging bag to take home and wash.

"See you tomorrow," Nora said. "I'll pray for you tonight that you find some beginnings of peace with Sharon's death. As an experienced nurse, please listen to me: Come back to work tomorrow. Don't call in. I promise you that facing the job tomorrow is the best thing you can do. Your colleagues are here for you."

We walked to the parking lot together. I held it together until I was in the car.

Chapter Thirty

"No nurses training is of any use unless
one can learn to feel...."
Florence Nightingale

In a teary daze, I drove home, somehow, making it into my mom's kitchen. She looked up. "I saved some tacos for you, honey. Do you want...Kit, what's the matter? Oh honey, what happened? Are you OK? Are you hurt?"

She turned off the stove and gathered me in her arms. We stumbled over to the kitchen table and sat down.

I cried, and soon Dad and Kai were in the kitchen holding me or patting me. They held me and told me everything was going to be OK while I raged against the unfairness of it all. I told them everything that had happened. I was so grateful to have them. Their love and concern were just what I needed.

Chapter Thirty-One

Wrecked Ruminations

Oh, God, I'm so scared and sad and sick and scared. My first death happened today. It was awful. Like a slasher movie. So much blood and so many things to do to try to save her. Nothing worked. She could have been my big sister. Her husband is bereft. And Dr. Billy let Nora know I was an incompetent boob. He's right, I know. At least now I have information from someone who knows. I can't do this. Maybe I could learn how to do the technical stuff, but I care too much. I can't remember the technical stuff and pretend I don't care about my patient. Nora has the guts for nursing. She can cry and then turn around as nothing happened and do her work. That's crazy. If she knows empathy as someone's pain in my heart, then how does she put her heart on a shelf when she's performing procedures and talking to families? I only have tomorrow left in the ICU. Maybe I'll go to work. Maybe I'll just go in later with my resignation letter. I can't stand this. Please help.

I closed the journal and climbed into bed. Trying to remember something normal and comforting, I prayed, Now I lay me down to sleep, I pray the Lord my soul to keep, if I wake to another day, I pray the Lord to tend my ways. Amen."

Chapter Thirty-Two

"We live together: let us live for each other's comfort."
Florence Nightingale

The following day, I did go to work, and Nora was in the locker room when I arrived.

"How are you doing? Yesterday was a rough day. Even I was flapped. To be a new nurse and see all that blood and witness a death must have knocked your socks off," said Nora.

"I'm OK, I guess. I think I scared my little brother. Didn't sleep very well. Every time I closed my eyes, I saw the look on Mark's face when he saw his wife. My mom and dad let me talk and cry for a long time last night when I got home. That helped a lot. I know they didn't know what to say, but I am so glad they just kept quiet and let me talk."

Nora nodded in understanding. "If you need to talk, let me know. I'm here for you. I know what it's like. Chaplain Harrison's emotional first aid is a good start. He'll come back today and set up a time for you and me to do a formal session, so we continue to process our feelings. They call it debriefing."

"Thank you so much, Nora. You're helping me right now. I'm ready to get back to work," I said as I headed toward Jay.

My hospital phone dinged with a text message from Susan. *The TMH grapevine is alive and well. I heard you had a horrific day yesterday. I'm free this evening and need some new fabric. Want to meet at Sew after work and talk?*

Yes Please! See you at 8:00. That'll give us an hour before they close.

We can solve a lot of the world's problems in an hour. See you then.

Chaplain Harrison was good to his word. He made an appointment and came to ICU that day. Lucy made sure that our patients were covered by other staff so that Nora and I had a chance to review again what had happened during those traumatic few hours.

Chaplain Harrison said little while we talked. That is, I did almost all the talking. He sat back when we finished. "Thank you very much for allowing me to hear your feelings about this experience. I don't expect this to be the last time you talk about your emotions. Sharon's bleeding and the tragic outcome were especially hard for you, Kit, I would think. I understand this was the first time since you became an RN that one of your patients died."

I nodded. "It's just so unfair. I know I've said that before, but it is. I keep thinking about what I could have done differently. Should I even consider working in such a high-stress area as ICU? Am I cut out to be a nurse?"

I'm glad you've thought through yesterday's events. Nora said, "One thing I learned a long time ago, Kit, is that we nurses tend to blame ourselves when patients don't do well. It's true that we absolutely should think about and evaluate our own practice. But, and this is a crucial point to understand, sometimes we have to admit there was nothing more we could have done."

"Then if it wasn't my fault or your fault, whose was it? Where was God in all this? That makes me the angriest of all. I guess God is simply fine with Sharon dying and leaving her husband. They'll never have a family. And her mom has lost her daughter. She wasn't even around to show her love in her last hours. Tell me, what's fair about that?"

"You're right," said Chaplain Harrison. "This is important enough to be angry about. None of this is fair. I promise not to blow smoke at you and tell you pious clichés. I won't tell you that God wanted to give Mark and Sharon's mom a trial to teach them something. I certainly won't tell you that this was meant to be. I believe that God is as sad as we are that Sharon died. Maybe more since I think he loves us more than we know how to love others.

"Patients don't always respond the way we hope they will. We can only stay informed and alert and offer emotional support to families as they go through this. If we take these situations personally, we set ourselves up to either indifferent or burned out. Evaluating what happened is incredibly important to learn, but just as important is taking care of ourselves. We need to refill our emotional reserves, so we have the energy to continue helping."

I sighed. "OK, Well. Thank you for coming here, Chaplain Harrison. When we covered Grief and Loss in school, I didn't understand how much this hurts nurses. Lots to think about. Thank you, Nora, too. I'm meeting Susan, my night residency mentor, tonight after work to help me process this. I'd better get back. Last day in ICU. Whoopee."

"I'm here in the hospital if you ever want to talk more," said Chaplain Harrison.

Nora helped sum up our time. "The first situation like this is tough for a new nurse, and this was about as bad as it gets. Jay and I are here to offer tons of support. I'm glad you have Susan to talk to too. She and I go a long way back to our own nurse residencies, and I know she understands. It takes time. It'll seem like forever, but be patient."

She sighed and patted me on the arm. "C'mon, Kit. Let's get back. They'll send out the search party soon." With that, we returned to ICU and our patients.

I had had my first lesson in compartmentalizing: taking a brief time to begin recovery from an awful patient situation and then turning my full attention to care for those who were counting on me. I wondered, How do nurses do this day after day without turning into blithering idiots?

Chapter Thirty-three

There is no end in what we may be learning every day.
Florence Nightingale

S usan and I had met a couple of times at the quilting shop. It seemed that crafting helped me when I got upset. My head calmed when I was doing something with my hands. You'd think I would be a craft ninja after the weeks I've been through in this nurse residency.

But no. Not true. I still felt like such an anomaly as a nurse. People tried to reassure me, but I was pretty sure that no successful nurse had ever been as heartbroken as I've been over a patient's death or as overwhelmed with so much information not covered in her nursing program. Susan seemed to understand right away.

After listening to my rambling story, she put down one of the bolts of fabric she was considering. She looked directly at me and said, "I'm sorry to tell you this, but you're not that special. Every single nurse I know has gone through the feelings you have."

"You can't expect a nursing program to teach you something that has to be experienced," said Susan. "Please listen. See if this doesn't sound like things you've been hearing from your mentors and your nurse Gram. Love of people is necessary to stay in nursing and not become a burned-out wreck. I mean, love, as in caring and allowing people to live their lives the way they choose. Look Kit. We support and affirm what people are going through. It's when we witness suffering that we, as nurses, act.

"Empathy is simple enough: It's the identification of another person's feelings and accepting those feelings as legitimate. Empathy doesn't mean we ignore suffering or take it casually like 'too bad for you.' We are to make informed and kind-hearted actions to alleviate suffering. That's compassion or caring.

"A healthy nurse learns to use empathy and compassion as a positive connection to patients. Compassion and empathy don't make a nurse softer or more emotional or crazy. Compassion and empathy create a more resilient nurse able to bounce back after taking care of the toughest patient situations.

"You've discovered a big idea, though. Nurses have to take care of themselves with stress-relieving actions. And we have to use stress-relieving techniques often and purposefully. Having a plan helps. Knowing other nurses you trust will help you talk and get support when you have problems."

"So, how do nurses know if they could be going down the wrong path?"

"Well, you and I talking this out is a good starting point. Stick with peers that you trust. It's part of self-care and will save your behind in nursing. I'll tell you what I think is a bigger problem than what you call 'caring too much.' It's when nurses are too busy to find out about who the people are who we're caring for. When we can't empathize and show compassion because we're too busy or don't take the time for ourselves, then we burn out."

Right there, in the batik fabric aisle, I thought about bouncing back from caring for suffering people. I'd never thought that wanting to control or deeply wanting to help could interfere with a patient's recovery. I'd seen nurses talking to patients and family members in ways meant to set them right when they didn't talk or behave in a good enough way. How were people supposed to know how their behavior affected their health if we didn't point it out to them? Nicely, of course. Something was a little off about that reasoning, but I didn't know why.

The conversation got so philosophical that Susan said, "You'd think we had all the answers to hear us talk. We should call ourselves Sew it All!

"Let's talk about this some more another day. You'll find our Thursday Sip group to be fantastic. They are just like me. We've been around the block in nursing and have an opinion about everything. We see and hear things that nobody would choose to experience, and we have to stick together so we can go on. Thanks for the conversation and for helping me pick out the blue and teal pieces. Any better now?"

"You know, I think I am a little better. Thanks," I said.

"Thanks to you too," said Susan as we walked to our cars. "We will keep each other as sane as we can! See you, Thursday Nurse!"

Chapter Thirty-Four

Responsiveness Ruminations

I'm getting better at seeing when I'm getting tangled up with my caring attitudes. When I want to control the other person's response to my care, I'm slipping into getting too close to the patient's situation. When I feel disappointed in how a patient is acting or if I feel sympathy (rather than empathy) to their situation, I know that I'm judging them based on what I think they ought to do. It's crazy to see how tired and stressed I could get if patients don't act in the way I believe is morally right or don't get well after my best nursing efforts. I used to think that if I identified with people's suffering, then I'd burn out. I remember what Nora said, "Empathy is your pain in my heart." That's the kind of feeling toward suffering that makes me want to act and help. But my help has to be given with no preconditions. If I think that the person's health has to be done the way I want it done, I can't help. When Sharon died, I felt like I cared too much. That wasn't what was going on. What was going on was that I wanted Sharon's husband to let me take over and control what happened with their situation. It wasn't caring too much; it was fear and pity. Gigantic difference. Later. Probably.

Chapter Thirty-Five

"The martyr sacrifices themselves entirely in vain.
Or, rather in vain; for they make the selfish more
selfish, the lazy more lazy, the narrow, narrower."
Florence Nightingale

Just getting to Sip and Stitch turned into a crazy struggle at
home. Mom was thrilled that I had been included in this regular get-together. At dinner, she exclaimed, "It's wonderful to be
invited to this party. Oh, you'll impress them so much, Kit. They
will all want to be your friend."

I looked at Dad and Maddy, and Kai. Kai was dishing out a
second helping of scalloped potatoes and didn't appear to think
anything was amiss. Dad shrugged his shoulders and ate some
salad to hide his grin, and Maddy said, "Oh yeah, Kit. You're
going to be a real hit at the party. Everybody will want to be
friends with you. You're just so wonderful. Oh my! I wish I
could be there too."

"Shut up, Matthew," I muttered in his direction. Mom
doesn't like the phrase "shut up," so I glared at him too so he
would be sure to get my message.

"You can't go to a party without taking something for the
hostess. I made some Nuts and Bolts. You can take a little tin."

Nuts and Bolts is mom's recipe. It includes dry rice cereal,
pita chips, pretzel sticks, peanuts, and chocolate chips coated in
peanut butter and covered with confectioners' sugar. It is one
of the unhealthiest things that a person could consume and is

utterly delicious. I didn't need to be talked into taking some to Susan's.

I arrived at Susan's house right at 7:00 pm and was not the first person there. The sound of laughter through the screen door was encouraging.

"Oh look, it's Kit!" said Susan. She walked me through the house to the kitchen and adjoining family room. There were about five women and one man in the room. Each person had some project in their laps, a glass of something, and a plate of cheese and crackers on TV tables scattered around the room. I handed the Nuts and Bolts to Susan, and the guy exclaimed, "Oh my gosh! I love that stuff. Just pass it over here, Susan!" With that promising beginning, I found a seat, opened a wine cooler, and set out my quilt square.

"So, how's it going in residency, Kit? By the way, I'm Patrick. I teach nursing at the community college, but to keep up my nursing skills, I work every other weekend nights."

"Hi, Patrick. Residency is going along OK."

Barb Mazur waved at me from across the room. She held up a knitting project and said, "Patrick, Kit is coming along just fine."

I blushed. "Thanks, Barb. My day shift mentor," I offered as (probably) an unnecessary explanation.

"I remember residency being so awful," said a woman sitting next to me. "I could never get anything straight. It's a wonder they hired me at the end. I'm Rosie."

Nearly everyone in the room smiled at me and then continued talking to each other.

"I'm so glad to hear you say that, Rosie," I said. "I'm beginning to think I won't ever get organized. My biggest problem, other than getting out on time, is finding time to talk to patients."

"Why aren't you talking to patients?" asked Rosie.

"Well, I do, but I don't have time to engage with them, so they know I care and empathize," I explained. "Then when I hear some of the problems they have, I feel so bad for them and worry even more that I'm not doing enough for them."

"I couldn't help overhearing. I remember wanting to be the kind of nurse I could be when I only had one or two patients and no other unit responsibilities. Rosie and I went through residency together five years ago. We nearly ran away and joined the circus about three months into residency. I'm Diane."

"Oh, that's so true. We believed that a high wire acrobat probably had it easier than we did. Some of those days would try the patience of a saint," said Rosie with a bark of laughter. "Tell her what we finally did!"

"Well," began Diane, "We began with cheesecloth and then progressed to circles. Honestly, once we got emotions out of our heads and worked together, it clicked."

"I remember this story," said Patrick. "Didn't you guys present this at a nursing conference in San Davers?"

"Yes," said Susan. "That's right, they did." The group clapped.

Diane gave a slight head bow of acknowledgment and went on, "When we address patient needs, we recognize we can't do everything for them. So, we allow the nursing-centered issues to permeate the cheesecloth and leave our feelings of powerlessness on the other side."

"Powerlessness is a good word. So is guilt. Leave them trapped in the cheesecloth," said Rosie. "They don't help the patient and only give us bad dreams."

"We shouldn't want to do everything for people anyway. It's not good to make people dependent on us. Our job is to help them learn to help themselves," added Patrick.

"Yep, so here is what Rosie and I did after we figured out that we needed to learn how to care for patients without getting emotionally trapped," said Diane, changing her thread color.

"Susan and I talked about referrals when I was on nights," I volunteered.

"Yep. Referrals to other clinics or community agencies can be good for some people, and others need help learning self-care. You know, you're not going home with patients. Anyway, as Patrick said, it's not respectful to do everything for patients," said Diane.

"Drum roll, please. The Circles!" said Rosie.

"OK, look. There are three big things you have to learn in residency. First Circle is Management of your time, Second Circle is Management of patient care, and Third Circle is Management of yourself." Three circles. In everyday nursing life that means Circle #1: take report, write the first six things that need to be done, then get any 8:00 am meds and pass them while you're checking in on your assigned patients. Keep your eye on your watch. It may seem supremely stressful at first, but it becomes a habit fast," Diane said and then gave a go-ahead gesture to Rosie.

"The second circle is Management of Patient Care. In residency, there are two things to focus on. First, practice technical skills to be safe, competent, and efficient. Never confuse efficiency with sloppiness. You want to be quick and good. The second is to practice quick, focused communication. Almost simultaneously, you will greet every patient with a smile and eye contact. Tell them who the heck you are. Use your hand to touch their shoulder or arm or hand, ask questions about their perceptions of their progress, listen to and accept the answer and tell them what you're going to do next."

Diane grinned and said, "The third circle is our favorite. We use the phrase always mentioned in emergency instructions on planes."

"Apply the oxygen mask to yourself before you help others," Rosie and Diane said in unison.

"Take care of yourself, so you have the stamina and thinking ability to care for others," concluded Diane.

All around the room, nurses started to give their Management of Self tips. "Sip and Stitch is my oxygen," "Yoga is mine," "My piano lessons," "Quilting," "Baking."

"As the nursing faculty member here, I feel like I have to say something to Kit. These are all creative and social outlets. See?"

"Yes, I see. Thank you for helping me help myself!" I exclaimed.

"We like S&S so much because nurse friendships are a special kind of friendship," said Susan.

"That's right," said Rosie. "It's a 'let me help you clean up your poopy patient who also just threw up' kind of friendship!"

"Once we got emotions out of our heads and worked together, things worked out," said Diane. "It was the interactions, the social contact that finally solved the problem."

I felt buoyed when I left. Little did I know there was still more good news.

When I turned on the phone in the car at 9:30 pm, there were four messages from Hannah. "Call me." "Where are you?" "Is your battery dead?" "Here's the flyer. Now call me!"

The flyer was a stunning color picture of Chateaux Bordeaux. It said, *"Halloween Open House this Saturday and Sunday. See our Boo-tiful apartments and amenities. Spook-tacular move-in specials. Park all brooms in the Lobby."*

I called Hannah! "I'm going! You are the best to have seen this and send it to me."

"I was staging the lobby and saw the flyer," Hannah said excitedly. "Oh Kit, wait until you see their apartment called the "Small One Bedroom. It's got a French balcony!"

"I'm going for sure on Saturday. The whole family will likely troop along, so do you want to come too?"

"Call me when you're finished. I've got a bathroom remodel job. Business is picking up!"

"It sure sounds like it is," I agreed. "Proud of you, my friend."

Chapter Thirty-Six

"Never underestimate the healing effects of beauty."
Florence Nightingale

I had Saturday off. This was important for two reasons: Football and Freedom. The football game between Trail State University, my alma mater, and Western Ohio University was scheduled for 4:00 pm. This is THE football game every year for TSU and WOU. The rivalry between the schools has run deep for over 100 years. My family planned a cookout, and Mom made pounds of trail mix, the official TSU school snack. Trail State had a great football team in 2018. Of course, they always have a great football team, but the team was tremendously great this year. We were going to beat WOU hollow! We were ready. This year, it was an away game, so none of us was attending in person.

I planned to visit Chateau Bordeaux in the morning and see if Hannah's information proved true. I told Maddy that I would go alone to their open house at 10:00 am. I just wanted to find out if their deals were that great. If it sounded OK, then I'd come back and ask mom and dad to go and look—plenty of time before the 4:00 pm kick-off.

Just as an aside, when will I ever learn? If you want to keep a secret, don't tell anyone in my family. Anyone. Maddy's loose lips resulted in the entire family waiting precisely at 10:00 am by my car. I mean the whole family—even Teddy, who doesn't live there anymore. Gram, who came to watch The Game, was decked out in a bedazzled TSU sweatshirt and jeans. Everyone else was wearing some form of TSU gear. Teddy assigned everyone a car, and off we went. Heaven help me.

I won't bore you with the details, but the open house was beautiful. Hannah had done a great job designing the lobby's space with Halloween and Move-in Specials themes. The lobby is locked, so visitors have to ring to be allowed admission to the elevators and apartments—score one for safety. There was also a pool, exercise room, and laundry facilities if the apartment didn't come with a stackable washer and dryer. Trash pick-up was included in the rent. The renter paid for the parking garage, cable, and the electric bill for air conditioning, heat, lights, and internet.

Here is the final deal. There were two "specials." The efficiency or studio apartment was very cool and ridiculously small. It was cool because it came with a Murphy bed system. Get this. The unit moved back into the living area by touching a button, and a queen bed opened. It closed and became a wall when the bed wasn't in use. There was a bathroom with a gorgeous, tiled shower and a walk-in closet.

Teddy just sniffed in disdain. "You'd go crazy in such a place. Might as well live in a hotel room." Gram loved the Murphy bed system. Mom and Dad said nothing.

But. The small one-bedroom, although not much larger, seemed more spacious. There is a walk-in closet, an actual bedroom, and a living/kitchen/eating room. This was the apartment special I had come to see. A French Balcony was included, but I was chagrined to realize it was less Oo-La-La and more just a large window with an outside ledge. There was a wrought iron fence in front of the ledge. Clearly, I didn't know a French balcony from my ear. There might be room for a tiny plant on it. Stylish, I thought. The window, the only window in the apartment, gave good light. There was no washer and dryer unit, so I'd have to use the building's facilities. Or Mom and Dad's.

Get this. The Special was exactly that. It was $300.00 less per month than the usual rent for the <u>entire</u> first year. Underground parking was included for the first year too. This whole package was $325.00 less each month! Spooktacular for sure! Score 2 for safety and car protection from the elements. A two-year lease was required, but that was no problem. Right?

I wanted this apartment. I had been saving, and I had the security deposit money. I could afford it with the massive discount. I was going to get it and told everyone as much.

"Nice," said Kai.

"Not bad big sis," said Maddy.

"The price makes it possible for you to continue to save for a down payment on a house," said Planning Ahead Teddy. "You don't want to have to pay rent forever."

"Don't forget, you need to budget for new tires on the Civic this year," said Dad. "I saw you were coming up on 60,000 miles. Laundromats cost money, you know. Without a washer and dryer, you will need to budget for the laundry machines."

"There is no window in the bedroom. Did you notice that? You won't know if it's day or night," said Mom. "Although I suppose that's no big deal if you're sleeping. The big window will cost a lot for drapes or blinds. It's huge. You'll have to get some that let light in, but you have to be careful; no one should be able to when the lights are on. You don't want everyone looking at you."

"Kit, it is so nice," said Gram. "This is one of the most pleasant small apartments I've ever seen. If you're sure you can afford it, I say go for it! I'll help you shop for a window treatment. Housewarming gift from me."

I ignored Teddy, rolled my eyes at mom's bedroom window and voyeur comments, told Dad that I would be sure to get new tires before I moved in and would save quarters to stay clean. Gram got hugs and kisses.

So, I made the best grown-up decision of my young life and got the apartment. I paid the security deposit, and the two-year lease began on November 10, 2018. All the way home, I sang the chorus to Richie Haven's hippie song *Freedom*.

We beat WOU 21-17.

Chapter Thirty-Seven

Respite Ruminations

I've moved into my glorious new apartment. It seems like I can write more now that I'm not looking over my shoulder to be sure no family journal spies are watching me. Am I being too vain to love my apartment? Sometimes I am flat out overwhelmed with gratitude for the support I've had since I moved back to Thompson. The nurses who have stuck with me told me I'm normal and to keep going...don't quit. My mom and dad who held me while I cried when Sharon died. Chaplain Harrison who admitted that he didn't have all the answers to life and death questions but gave me just enough spiritual support to keep going. No pontificating, but he knew when to talk and when to listen. Nursing is so spiritual. Hardly an original thought, but now when I say my soul was hurt and patched up by those who understand, I believe it.

I've got one more month of residency, and since I'm now paying rent and washer and dryer money, I guess I'll stay in nursing. Thank heavens for my S&S friends. They learned about my new apartment because I almost took out an ad in the TMH employee newsletter. They had a shower for me! Its theme was "Early Attic." Everyone brought me things like pots and pans, full-sized sheets, kitchen towels, bath towels, and many other household things they no longer needed but were in great shape. They thanked me for helping them clean out their closets, and I got some fantastic items. I got the biggest bang out of the vintage

CorningWare from the older nurses. Everyone must have had pots and skillets with blue cornflowers in the day. The stuff certainly holds up; it looked new. There was even furniture. Patrick gave me a well-used coffee table that he said he was delighted to donate. What a blast. They all wanted to know how the last few nurse residency weeks were going. I told them that Cheesecloth *was my motto, and they all cheered.*

Gram and I found out that vertical blinds came in the size of my window, and she bought me a soft grey set. No one can see through them when they're closed.

Hannah and her mom helped me find some awesome furniture from the consignment shop. A bistro table with two chairs, a small sectional that was practically new from a couple who were downsizing, and asked Hannah to find someone who would pay $100.00 for it and two-floor lamps with tiffany-like glass shades. It seems as though no one is using "good china" or "good silverware" anymore, so a fancy china service for 12 with stainless silverware and steak knives was available for $50.00 total! It was nice to get the Family Discount at the consignment shop! I bought a full-sized bed and frame, mainly because any size bigger wouldn't fit in the bedroom without being shoved up against both walls. A dresser, a small table, and another lamp from the consignment shop completed my bedroom layout. I've saved the best for last. The consignment store had a sunburst mirror just like Gram gave away years ago. Hannah said it would help my living/eating/kitchen area look larger by reflecting light. Sold!

While I was in San Davers for the blinds, Mary, Erin, and I went to IKEA, where I got a duvet cover and a supremely cool print that looked like a window opening to a cobblestone street. My bedroom now has a window.

OK, I'm finished waxing poetic about my new apartment— one more thing. My car thinks it has died and gone to heaven to be in a covered garage every night. OK. One more last thing.

Washers and dryers cost dollars, not quarters, these days. Dad and Mom were shocked, and Mary and Erin said, "duh!"

OK. I'm done talking about the apartment. For now. I still can't believe I got what I dreamed about. That never happens. My pastor thinks I've had some sort of crisis or something. I've shown up for church every Sunday since the Chateau Bordeaux Open House! It's not a crisis, Pastor Linda. It's thankfulness. I can't believe this happened. I'm trying not to get too carried away. I haven't signed up to teach Sunday School or some crazy idea like that!

ICU orientation finished well enough. I did like it there and learned many, many things about communication that is caring but brief. I don't want to be loved by patients anymore. I'm much more willing to listen and understand the absolute heartbreak of critical illness. Doing nursing technical skills correctly and staying alert to changes in patient conditions is slowly taking my attention off me and onto my patients. Jay and Nora were truly role models. I'm going back to 3 North for the last month of residency, and then, who knows. I'll need to decide where I want to work and apply for an open position. There is no doubt that nurses are needed on almost every unit, except OB and Surgery. My mentor evaluations have been good, so I think I'll get hired.

Amanda has never taken to ICU or adult medical surgical nursing. That's putting it mildly. She hated inpatient bedside nursing. Her mentors thought she had the potential to be an asset to nursing if she was in the right practice area. Human Resources decided to offer her last residency month in the outpatient clinics rather than returning to 3 South. She's delighted and so am I because she and I are becoming friends. Last night after work, I invited Amanda to see my Very Magnificent Apartment and celebrate her move to the outpatient clinics. Right after we toasted her good fortune, and she dutifully exclaimed compliments over my digs, the doorbell rang at the locked lobby door.

It was Maddy. He had some time and came to hang some pictures and my most fabulous sunburst mirror. I buzzed him in. Now, get this. When Maddy saw Amanda, he honest-to-goodness stopped in his tracks. I started to say, "Hey, Maddy, this is Amanda, someone I work with." No need for that kind of etiquette. Maddy and Amanda seemed almost stunned, looking at each other. I swear if it had been a movie, there would have been violins and flutes playing a soap opera love melody in the background. Amanda stayed until he finished my mirror and pictures. Then, ever the gentleman, Maddy walked her to her car. They've been dating ever since. Straight-Up-Stunner. I suppose I should start calling him Matt, right? Nah.

Chapter Thirty-Eight

"We are volunteers. Don't let us forget that."
Florence Nightingale

I spent the last four weeks of nurse residency back on 3 North. I was glad to be back. It was familiar, and the routine felt more manageable than when I left for the ICU rotation. By reminding myself of cheesecloth and focusing on the three circles. I hoped this last month of residency would be more centered. Thank you, Diane and Rosie!

While I was in ICU residency, Emily had implemented on-call for the 3 North RNs. She had a small group of day and night RNs work with her to make the requirement as fair as possible.

The nursing shortage was beginning to be felt acutely on 3 North. Everyone was working at nearly total capacity. There was at least one open position on every shift, and it was getting more difficult to convince nurses to work extra shifts when there were call-ins.

Nurses would be paid a small stipend for on-call hours. If called in, they would receive regular salary; if working over 80 hours in a two-week pay period, overtime pay at time and one-half would kick in.

We had an obligation to sign up for 36 on-call hours each month. On-call hours were six or 12 hours in length. The total on-call hours required were 12 weekend hours on a weekend we were not scheduled to work and 24 hours during the week each month. Sign-up for on-call hours was fluid and scheduled online. A nurse could sign up months in advance for on-call shifts to respect personal life. Nurses couldn't change their on-call choices after the last Saturday of the previous pay period unless they found a replacement. Emily kept a close eye on the schedule to ensure that the next four weeks were fairly distributed. We were able to sign up for more than the requirement, and so for a while, at least, some eager beavers were signing up for extra on-call. The only stipulation was that scheduling oneself for purposeful overtime had to be approved by Emily. I was not excited about on-call because I thought that the chance of being called in was fairly high since there were open positions. The entire TSU system, not just TMH, was affected. The Recruitment Department offered sign-on bonus incentives to experienced RNs, and the six-month nurse residency became a standard part of the job offer to all new graduates. Managers were trying to convince older nurses not to retire yet and self-scheduling the shifts we wanted to work (within parameters) became more common. Peer pressure was on too. Nurses were pointedly asked to carefully consider whether or not they were really sick before calling in or whether they simply wanted a "mental health day" off.

The hospital seemed to be doing a fair bit to address the nursing shortage, so while I wasn't openly critical, I was worried. The hospital administration made their message clear: Patients needed care, and as nurses, we signed up for this responsibility. I had one more month before residency ended, and then, on-call would become part of my life too.

Chapter Thirty-Nine

**"Remember, the Nurse is wanted most by the most
helpless & often most disagreeable cases; in one sense,
there is no credit in nursing pleasant patients."**
Florence Nightingale

O n my first Saturday back on 3 North, it seemed as though
nursing was out to get me. The unit was packed. For every
discharge planned that day, at least one patient needed to be
transferred from the ICU. One of the nurses called in sick on
the night shift, so the RN report was not specific on the newest
admissions. Tanya, my favorite CNA, had the weekend off for
a family event. In her place was Jacob Minski, a student nurse
who worked as a nursing assistant every other weekend at TMH
to get some practical hospital experience. Sophia Lumberger
was the other RN on my wing. Thank goodness Barb agreed to
work an extra shift and was the charge nurse.

I started my morning rounds to evaluate my six assigned
patients. Deb Gill had been readmitted. I remembered her from
ICU and was curious how she recovered post head injury and
fractured femur. A concussion was discovered in the diagnostic
workup, and seizures were an unfortunate complication. Deb had
been home for about a week. For the past few days, she had been
suffering from incapacitating headaches. She was admitted from
the ED last evening. Her nursing priority was safety and risk
reduction because of her history of seizures and fractured right
leg. She had a full leg cast and required assistance to turn in bed,

especially moving from the bed. Family support and education regarding seizure precautions, circulation checks, and medications at home were also priorities. During report, the nurse said Deb needed frequent comforting and reminding to use her button to get out of bed. She had fallen in the night, and an incident report was completed. The nurse practitioner from the ED examined her. No immediate injury was noted, and the neurologist was notified. This morning, further evaluation was planned.

I decided to see Deb first. She smiled at me when I came into the room.

"Hi, honey," she said cheerfully, "What a bad night I had. They told me I fell. I'm fine, really, but for a minute there, they said I didn't know where I was."

Confusion is common in older patients at night. This is especially a problem with those patients who have neurological issues. Deb didn't recognize me from the ICU, which was not surprising. She was pretty out of it right after the accident. I explained that sometimes nighttime can be disorienting in a hospital, but that injuries, such as her fall, were taken very seriously. She could expect further evaluation from her neurologist and hospital safety personnel today.

Deb's neuro assessment showed equal and reactive pupils, a strong hand grasp on both sides, and no facial drooping. Deb's speech was clear; she knew where she was and said she did not have a headache. Vital signs were within the range noted on the night shift. I was satisfied that Deb most likely had some confusion during the night that dissipated when daylight came. She nodded, understanding that even though the hospital bed was in the lowest position and the side rails were down, it would be best for her to call for help if she needed to use the restroom or wanted to get up for any reason.

"I understand completely, honey. Here's my call button, see? I know you're just doing your job, and even though I'm perfectly fine, I promise to call you if I want to get up."

What a sweet woman, I thought and went to the next room. Jacob, the CNA, was talking to Caleb Lang, a young man who had been admitted for reconstructive surgery on his hand. Last evening while doing carpentry work in his basement, his hand slipped on a circular saw and made a deep cut. He was NPO; nothing permitted to eat or drink, so that he would be ready for surgery. The plastic surgeon from University Hospital was coming this morning to repair the deep damage. Jacob's wrists had strong radial pulses, he had feeling in both hands, his nail bed color was pink, and the dressing was dry with no drainage.

I felt Jacob follow me out of the room. "I have a question, Kit. Caleb told me that he takes pot to relax because he has a lot of stress in his life. He says he has a prescription for medical marijuana. Does that need to go on his medication sheet? It's not there now."

"That's a great question, Jacob. Yes, marijuana should be on his medication sheet. Thanks for noticing. The legal use of medical marijuana is relatively new in the state, you know. In any case, when getting a medication inventory, nurses need to ask about all taken medicines. We need to know the meds from a prescription and those over the counter. I'll make a note to verify his prescription with the physician and be sure that the surgeon knows."

How did that get missed? We had multiple in-services and written policies sent to our emails, and even a reminder note on our nurse's restroom door at "eye level." There is just so much to remember.

While documenting Jacob's pot use in TIMES, I noticed that Sophia Lumberger was just then leaving the nurses' station after report. She seemed to have a lot of time to chat about her kids and things she had seen on social media. I run around like a crazy woman, and Sophia just goes casually through the day. She's cheerful, almost jolly sometimes, but seriously annoying most of the time. If I had heard Sophia introduce herself once as "Lumberger, like stinky cheese, you know?" I had heard it a hundred times. Wait. Wait. Here's the punchline. "Actually, I am like stinky cheese. I get better with age! Bahahaha."

So breathtakingly original, right? Get some work done, Stinky Cheese.

With no warning, a crashing sound came from my assigned side of the hall. "Heeeelllpp," yelled a woman. Nurses appeared from all over the unit and converged in Deb Gill's room. She was tangled in her bedsheet and screaming. "Get away from me, you people, or I'll call the police! I can see you coming to get me. Heeelllpp!"

I moved toward her, calmly calling her by name. "Deb, you're in the hospital, and you've fallen out of the bed. Let me help you."

"OK, honey," said the now sweet Deb.

Jacob and I put our arms around her and started to help her stand.

"You are trying to kill me!" she shouted, and then...bit me firmly in the lower arm!

Another nurse said, "I'll call the Code Gray."

The announcement of help requested for a combative person began overhead:

"ATTENTION THOMPSON MEMORIAL HOSPITAL, CODE GRAY ROOM 318

"ATTENTION THOMPSON MEMORIAL HOSPITAL, CODE GRAY ROOM 318

"ATTENTION THOMPSON MEMORIAL HOSPITAL, CODE GRAY ROOM 318"

Security officers and the physician on call arrived quickly and helped restore a safe and calmer environment. Deb Gill continued to shout with obscenities mixed in with her paranoiac pleas for help. Orders were received for sedation, and the physician ordered a soft restraint that was the safest and least limiting restriction. An order was written for a brain CT. A security officer was directed to stay with Mrs. Gill until she could be moved to a setting that allowed closer direct observation.

The house supervisor took me aside. "Well, the skin on your arm is broken. She bit you quite hard, didn't she? What a pile of ...anyway, I'm sorry. You'll go to the ED for evaluation. The incident report will be completed there. Are you OK with going alone? Barb will reassign your patients until you're back."

I heard Barb ask the unit clerk Mary Westfield to call the RN on call.

Of course, I had to wait in the ED since the emergency department was crowded and no rooms were immediately available. Once in an exam room, Dr. Brody Morgan introduced himself as one of today's ED physicians. He was thorough and kind.

"We're going to clean this up and lightly dress it," he explained. "It's not very deep, which is good. Human bites are very tricky. The human mouth has so many microorganisms that suturing bites is never done. The chance for serious infection is too great. In fact, the human mouth is so dirty that it would be better for you to be bit by a dog than kissed by your boyfriend." The joke has some truth to it and is incredibly old. I first heard it in Microbiology class in college, but I laughed today as though he was an original wit. Dr. Morgan was in charge of making sure I lived through this, and I didn't want to upset the guy.

"What about HIV? What about Hepatitis? Are you going to test my blood? I don't think the patient has either, but I want to be sure." I knew I was blabbing and didn't care one bit. "I checked her chart and didn't see any HIV or Hepatitis risk factors."

"Oh yes, we don't want to take any chances. We will be testing both you and the patient that bit you."

One of the ED nurses came in, and the bite was cleaned and lightly dressed. My tetanus vaccine and Hepatitis B status were verified as being up to date by Employee Health records. Because HIV, the human immunodeficiency virus, is spread by blood, and Deb Gill's bite had broken skin, a blood sample was drawn to test for Hepatitis B and HIV. Mrs. Gill would also have the same lab tests drawn.

I couldn't even process the thought of having HIV and Hepatitis B. The nurse explained it would be a few days before I'd know about the HIV and Hepatitis results compared with Mrs. Gill's lab studies.

I was released two hours after I arrived and returned to the unit. The rest of the shift passed as if in a blur. Everyone was helpful but kept their distance from me. The on-call nurse was happy to leave. I'll bet they were thinking, keep your distance from the seriously ticked-off nurse. Very compassionate, right?

Barb greeted me with a hug. "You OK, kiddo? This was a real nursing trial by fire day for you! I'm here if you need anything the rest of the day." That meant a lot.

Chapter Forty

Resentful Ruminations

I don't know why, but everybody is seriously ticking me off today. I do feel better when I write things down and "yell" in this journal. I'm more and more sure that I shouldn't be a nurse. There is never enough staff; I run around like a fool, the patients are so sick, there is never enough time to sufficiently take care of people and tell them what they need to know to take care of themselves when they go home. Today I had 10 minutes to remind a lady how to care for her congestive heart failure at home. That was all the time I had to help with a daily weight chart, review her diet plan and medication schedule. The dietitian saw her yesterday, but I'm sure she doesn't understand enough. And some of my co-workers are crazy nuts. Someone always asks me for help after they've been sitting around talking in the nurses' station. It seems some of them wait for me as I rush through there on my way to some other patient's need. Every day there is something I don't know. The other departments are so slow to respond to my requests. They say they're busy too. That's probably true but waiting for an hour for a STAT blood test is inexcusable. I told the lab supervisor too.

How can I be expected to run around like a waitress on New Year's Eve all day long PLUS also know the nuances of nursing care for health conditions and diseases while answering questions from every Tom, Doctor, Lab, Dietary, visitor, Dick, and Harry? It's impossible. And did I mention I got BITTEN by a patient today? Bitten. By a person who thought I was trying to kill her. And did I mention I have to wait to see if the patient has HIV? Or Hepatitis B? And that I had to go back to work (or else take vacation time) after getting treated for a HUMAN BITE.

Mom thought this kind of violence toward a nurse was a real oddity. Her advice was to let somebody in charge know about it. Are you kidding me? What a grand idea! I almost laughed out loud. I'm pretty sure the incident report and the ED report will reach the right people. I could only tell her that it was a good idea. I guess you could say Gram understood. She was sorry it happened, but I thought she'd be a little more sympathetic. The actual truth is, Gram felt sorry for my patient, the Biter. "It must be terrifying to be paranoid," she said.

"What about me? HIV? Hepatitis? Wound infection?" I asked her, absolutely incredulous at her insensitivity.

"Kit, honey, we signed up for this. Your patient didn't," she said.

It isn't common on 3 North, but we learned about patient violence in nursing school. Never thought I'd have to experience it first-hand. No pun intended. They don't pay me enough to get this kind of treatment.

It's not everybody. Susan and Barb are fantastic. Some of the others are too. I think I'm just in the wrong field. What do I want to do with my life, what do I want to do with nursing? The residency is almost over, and I'm supposed to apply for one of the open positions. ICU? 3 North? Neither one sounds good today. No pressure, though. There is rent to consider and all the other bills. I have to decide and apply by the end of the month. That gives me two whole weeks. God help me.

Chapter Forty-One

"There is so much talk about persons now-a-days. Everybody criticizes everybody. Everybody seems liable to be drawn into a current, against somebody, or in favour of ... pleasing herself, or getting promotion. If anyone gives way to all these distractions and has no root of calmness..., (she) will not find it in any Hospital or Home. "
Florence Nightingale

I needed my Gram. I didn't know what was wrong with me. I had a fantastic apartment, plus I had friends from work and outside nursing that I saw regularly. I continued to follow Rosie and Diane's cheesecloth and three circles survival tool; quilting and yoga are how I put the oxygen mask on me first. My family seemed to be behaving better now that I didn't have to see them every day and explain my every move.

Nurse residency was almost over, and Emily wanted to hire me. She said, and I quote, "You did fine enough in the nurse residency. Your ICU and 3 North mentor evaluations are satisfactory. You can apply for one of the 3 North open positions, and it will be OK."

Have you ever heard such a glowing recommendation? I am apparently a "fine enough" new nurse. It's OK if I apply for an open position. Seriously? If Emily wanted to be sure I was humble enough, her evaluation of Just-Good-Enough-Kit clinched it.

What was wrong? I looked forward to going to work. Every day something captured my attention and entertained my mind.

So why did I have crying jags on the way home because I still don't know enough? I'm not sure I want to work on 3 North. Maybe ICU would be better for my career. Mary and Erin had already finished their residency because they started two weeks earlier than I did. They were both working nights on a step-down thoracic unit at University Hospital. Nights nearly killed me in residency. Thinking about doing it forever is nauseating.

I decided that I was not prepared for the end of nurse residency. I thought the residency would never end, and yet Bang! It was nearly finished. Transition to applying for an open position came up way too fast. There was the on-call requirement bugging me too. It didn't sound like I could get a residency extension even if there were such a thing. TMH had spent money educating and training me and expected to get a competent nurse in return. Well, they're getting an OK one. I needed my Gram.

Gram had the next Wednesday off, and so did I. Her idea of a cure-all is a mani-pedi and facial. She told me to come to San Davers for lunch, a spa experience, a listening ear, and advice from a nurse that has "seen way too much but likes nursing anyway."

Gram had it planned down to the last detail. She and I sat next to each other for our hands and feet. My nails were beautifully shortened, filed, and polished with Sunrise Pink. My toes made me ridiculously happy when Purple Sparkle was applied. We even had side-by-side tables for the facial.

I never stopped talking. Gram nodded a little, said, "oh gosh yeah," and "isn't that the friggin' truth?" Mainly, she was silent and attentive.

Here's the gist of how I explained my dilemma to Gram: I didn't know enough, and TMH was about to let me loose without a mentor. I still got behind during every shift and had to hustle to catch up. But. The pay was good. I had a really sweet apartment and needed to keep working to pay the rent. But. Being on call would eat up some of my time off even though I might not be called in. Won't that make taking care of myself that much harder? But. Staffing is tight. There aren't enough nurses to go around. I think TMH would hire more, but I'm not sure how that's coming along. To hospital administration, money is so important. But. The extra money for on-call will come in handy. I just didn't know what to think or do. Honestly, there was so much to do every shift. Now, on-call meant that I might have to work even more. I liked the people I worked with. The S&S group was there for me and were now my friends. Here was the bottom line: I didn't think other jobs were this hard. My friend Hannah has her own interior design business, and she gets to set her own hours. She said she didn't have enough clients yet, so she still lived with her mom. She was her own boss, though. She doesn't have to worry about harming anyone by choosing the wrong color or sofa fabric. Not that I want to design kitchens or stage a house to sell, but that was not the point. "See? What should I do? This is just... just...overwhelming."

Gram sat up and smiled. She paid for both of our beauty treatments (I love my Gram), and we walked to the coffee shop. I have to admit that facial Gram got contained some powerful anti-aging properties. She looked great. I probably looked like a stressed-out banshee with nice skin.

"Everything you said is true, honey. Nursing is hard. It takes intelligence, a quick problem-solving mind, physical resilience, a desire to care with kindness, and cooperative communication skills," said Gram. "And then, there's the fun stuff that either makes a nurse or drives them away: a high tolerance for ambiguous situations and an ability to get along with those co-workers and patients who may be unmotivated, pretentious, and negative. Oh, Kit, nursing takes a tough spirit."

I laughed in relief. She understood. "Oh Gram, what should I do?"

"Do? What do you mean? It sounds like you can see some positive parts to your work. It's not all horrible. Kit. It's work.

Work is hard no matter what you do. That's why it's called Work and not Finally Fulfilled."

"Come on, Gram. Nurses work harder than teachers or interior designers or coffee shop owners."

"I don't know that, Kit. I admit that nurses work pretty consistently for a full shift without much downtime. But that's the nature of the professional role at the bedside. Nothing will change that if you do it right. Nurses don't have the same concerns as teachers, interior designers, and coffee shop owners, so comparing isn't fair. Do you want to do those things?"

"Heck no. It's just that nursing is so much harder than I thought it would be. My S&S friends tell me that being a martyr isn't becoming, and it's not as though I'm alone. Get off the cross, one of them told me!"

"Your friends are right, and you're lucky to have people who tell you the unvarnished truth. My dear sweet Kit. You are trying to evaluate your practice on the same level as a nurse with years more experience. It takes at least…at least Kit…10,000 hours to become an expert bedside nurse. That's over five years."

"Crap," I said.

"Well said."

"I'm going to apply for one of the 3 North jobs and keep trying to be the nurse I want to be."

"OK. I like that decision. As a nurse who immodestly calls herself an expert critical care nurse, I can tell you the truth. Remember that you have friends and family that will listen and help you. Don't stop talking to us and journaling. You're well on your way to becoming a godsend to every patient who has you as their nurse. You've already made a difference in the lives of some patients who never told you."

"Oh, Gram. I love you." I burst into tears.

"Go ahead and cry. Nursing is worth it. Then dry your eyes, finish your latte, and buck up! We need you."

Chapter Forty-Two

"The underlying principle of maintaining health is (for the nurse) to put the patient in a condition which is best for nature to act upon him or her and allows the patient to retain their energy or "vital powers" for use toward self-healing."
Florence Nightingale

Lydia was in charge today. It was one of the Monday federal holidays that hospitals don't formally recognize. I have to admit that the atmosphere was more relaxed than usual in morning report. Because of the holiday, there were no elective surgeries.

"Kit, Kevin Kendall's discharge was delayed yesterday," Susan began in the night shift report. "There is concern that he and his family need more education about his PICC IV line and wound care. There is some pressure from Utilization Management to have him discharged this morning. His insurance company has only approved his stay through today. We don't want him to stay if he can care for himself at home, and we don't want a readmission if he's discharged too early."

Susan rolled her eyes. "Honestly, sometimes I feel like most of my job is keeping insurance companies happy…which makes Emily happy…which makes Administration happy… which gives me less to stress about."

I agreed to give Kevin's discharge my #1 priority today and get him back home if at all possible. I hoped and prayed that I could get the Kendall family on board with his home care. It was often not a lack of intelligence but something else that prevented patients and families from showing they knew enough to go home. Kevin Kendall had diabetes and was in the hospital with a severe complication of the disease. He was overweight and was sedentary. According to his nursing history, Kevin's daily exercise seemed to be driving to work, designing computer-assisted architecture drawings, and driving home. He enjoyed playing cards and watching cable news. Kevin checked his blood sugar once daily and gave himself insulin once daily. More frequent blood sugar checks were needed to ensure he received the correct dose, type, and timing of insulin. Before hospitalization, his blood sugars were not in good control. Subsequently, he developed an infected leg ulcer caused by poor circulation and high blood sugar levels. He had a PICC IV line to give antibiotics twice each day at home and a wound care routine that needed to be completed twice each day. Blood sugars levels were to be checked four times each day, and insulin was to be given based on those readings. It was a lot to ask of a man and his family who had largely ignored a serious chronic disease. I suspected the family's fear of these medical treatments was delaying discharge.

After initial rounds, a quick review of labs, and passing 8:00 am meds, I knocked and walked into room 319. The TV was on to the local morning show and could be heard from the hallway. Kevin Kendall was enthusiastically eating his breakfast; his wife Lisa was enjoying a cup of coffee, and his teenage daughter Alexa was tapping into her phone, looking tremendously bored.

"Good morning, Kevin," I said, raising my voice over the TV.

"Hey, it's Kit. Look, honey, it's Kit. What's up with my favorite nurse?" Kevin boomed back.

"I wonder if you could turn down the TV, Kevin. I want to talk with you about going home today."

The TV was promptly shut off, and Lisa said, "I'm so glad you're here, Kit. Kevin wants to go home, but I cannot bring myself to do what they want me to do. Can't he stay here a little while longer?"

"Oh, that's a great idea," his daughter said. "Let's trap me here longer. This is so much fun."

"Alexa Joy!" Lisa exclaimed. "Your dad is sick, and we could make it worse by taking him home."

Kevin winked at me as though we were sharing a big secret in cahoots. "Yeah, her middle name is Joy. Go figure. Rather be with her friends than worry that I could lose my leg!"

"Well, Alexa, I kind of feel your pain," I said. "Being trapped in a hospital is no fun. Let's see if we can get your dad out of here."

Alexa rolled her eyes heavenward. "Thank you! A reasonable person!" She smiled a little and went back to her phone.

Yes indeed. Something going on that was more than just learning home care. I sat down in a chair facing Kevin and Lisa. Alexa looked at us out of the corner of her eye and then quickly tried to appear apathetic.

"It sounds like you're almost terrified to go home. Is there something that is making you especially worried?"

"The diabetes doctor came in on Saturday and read us the riot act," said Lisa tearing up. "I didn't know that Kevin could go blind or need his leg amputated if we didn't do things right. Kevin said he'd help, but the doctor made it clear that I was responsible for making sure he got better."

I was reasonably sure the endocrinologist intended to emphasize the importance of a family effort to control his diabetes at home. Obviously, Lisa heard that the doctor directed her to be the leader.

"That's a lot for one person to worry about," I said. "Let's talk about each thing that Kevin needs help with at home, how you can do a lot of this together, and see if we can make this a little more manageable."

Lisa and Kevin showed how they worked together to change the wound dressing and connect the antibiotic to the IV. They carefully followed sterile technique, used proper handwashing before and after each procedure, and properly bagged the soiled dressing for disposal. It was impressive.

"I have to be honest with you both," I said. "You do a wonderful job. What are you scared about the most?"

Kevin and Lisa looked at each other and, in unison, sighed in relief.

Kevin spoke first. "I guess we got a big shock from the doctor. I know that I didn't realize this sugar thing was such a big whoop."

Lisa looked directly at Kit. "His diet is my other worry. Kevin eats anything he wants whenever he wants. The dietitian said he needs to be much stricter about his diet and watch what he eats."

"Hey! A guy has to eat, and you know I like my beers during the game," Kevin said.

Lisa never lost eye contact with me. "He eats everything he wants, usually with seconds and thirds."

"I have been on this diabetes thing for a long time, and I know how to handle it."

"I know you do, Kevin. Tell 'your favorite nurse' how you handle it, see if she agrees with your plan of treatment."

"Look," Kevin said, "I eat what I want, within reason …"

"Who's reason?" Lisa asked.

"I eat what I want," Kevin said, "and before I go to bed and right before lunch, I drink a bunch of water to wash out my system and get rid of all the sugar."

I didn't know how to break it to the poor guy. He was acting as though he'd never heard a thing about diabetes. "Kevin, it doesn't quite work that way. What do you think causes diabetes, and why are the doctors prescribing the specific medications and diet? Do you know how you developed the leg ulcer?"

Kevin mumbled some answers.

"You can't flush out excess sugar by drinking a lot of water. It's the high sugar levels that caused the severe circulation problems that lead to the severe complication of your leg ulcer."

I went on, "Can you tell me why you think we're being such sticklers about monitoring blood sugar multiple times each day... giving insulin as prescribed for specific blood sugar levels,... eating a well-balanced lower-calorie balanced diet,... and daily exercise?"

Kevin looked down again while I was talking and muttered answers. He took a deep breath, shook his head, and quietly chuckled.

"OK. I know all this. I know that it isn't too much candy that caused my sugar problems. I know I should check my sugar before meals and before bed. I know I can sometimes have one beer, and two or three beers are bad for me. I know about the bad complications. I'm here, aren't I? I know. I know. I know!"

He began to talk with a mocking voice. "If you followed all the recommended medical treatments, why then you will feel better overall and drastically decrease further complications of your diabetes. Doesn't that sound like a great benefit?"

Then, in his regular voice, "Kit, I just hate this disease. I hate it and want it just to go away. I try to do what I can, but you're asking too much. I can't do it all."

Looking directly at Kevin, I said, "I'm not going to give you a pep talk Kevin. I bet you've heard enough of those. Your very amusing rendition of the diabetic "cheerleader" lecture showed me that! I admit that accepting a disease that gets involved with every single part of your life is worth getting mad about. It's a tough truth, but it's the real deal truth. If you want to feel better and get people off your back and get moving around like you used to, you'll have to come to some agreement with yourself to take care of yourself." He and I looked hard at each other, and we both sighed at the unfairness of it all.

"OK. I'll do more than just try this time. No promises. Thanks for your tough talk," he said.

Lisa grabbed Kevin's hand. "I'm an office manager and can organize almost anything. But the wound changes and the antibiotic, the diet and the four times a day sugars and insulin!" She sighed. "I wish we had some help at home."

"Now, there is some good news," I said. "With all the information you've been given, you may not remember that a nurse will visit you at home two times each week to be sure you're doing OK with the diet and insulin and wound treatment. I see in the notes that she is scheduled to see you tomorrow morning at 10:00 a.m. You should have her phone number if anything comes up too. Did the diabetes nurse come in?"

Lisa opened the bedside drawer and pulled out a stack of papers. "Uh, I don't know. Maybe."

We found the nurse's business card, where the appointment for tomorrow was written, and when to expect the antibiotics and dressings to be delivered to their home this afternoon by 5:00 pm. I circled the Diabetic Support Team information to remind Kevin and Lisa to ask if they could talk to other persons with diabetes who have had similar struggles with this challenging chronic disease.

"Hmmm. This is more organized than I realized. Don't worry, Kit. We will work hard at it this time," said Lisa.

Alexa Joy jumped up with a grin on her face. "Thanks, nurse, It's about time I can go home!"

I met Lydia in the nurses' station. "Good deal," said Lydia, "Let's get Kevin on his way. And, of course, going home is most important for Alexa. I can still remember being that age. I can't imagine being stuck in our unit, in our hard chairs, and being completely separated from the Cool Kids!"

"Oh yeah, it's tough to learn that life isn't all about you," I said. "It took me 23 years and a harrowing nurse residency to get a grip on that myself!"

"Nursing isn't for sissies, is it?" Lydia smiled and sighed, "You're going to be OK, Kit. I hope you stick with it."

Chapter Forty-Three

Residency Ruminations

I don't know if I'll be able to write anything coherent. Today was the last day of my nurse residency. What a crazy six months! I took in donuts from Weber's this morning to thank everyone for putting up with me on 3 North this year. I took a box over to ICU too. Candy and Jay stood by me at some of the most confusing times of my first year in nursing. Candy seemed unimpressed with the donuts, but Jay seemed thrilled. I think if Candy had been open and friendly, I would have wondered if I was in the wrong unit. She taught me a lot, and that's good enough.

So much went on from mid-June to mid-December. Barb deserves a medal for tolerating my know-it-all attitude. I still cringe when I think about suggesting atropine when my patient was in ventricular fibrillation. I'll never forget defibrillation then epinephrine. I heard Emily say that Susan has been assigned to mentor the new nurse resident. Jacob has been working as a CNA this year on some weekends; he starts on Monday. I like Jacob. If I can help him get through his first year, I will.

Speaking of Jacob. He told me about something that his grandmother told him. It was a quote from a guy named Dan Rather, a famous journalist on the national news as far back as the 1960s. He said, "If all the difficulties were known at the outset of a long journey, most of us would never start out at all." Amen to that, Mr. Rather!

I'm not so upset with nursing school anymore. They prepared me to take the NCLEX and pass it. They gave me a taste of what nursing is and, if I'd paid better attention, they warned me about some of the pitfalls and tough spots. They taught me to continue to learn. I was supposed to learn about the real world in my first job as a registered nurse. TMH taught me that you couldn't practice what you don't experience in nursing. They gave me so many chances to make rookie mistakes. Thank God for all of them. In the words of my Senior Nursing Projects Professor Dr. Mona Maye, "It's a continuum people. You learn things in the order you're supposed to learn them. If you're paying attention, that is. Pay attention, people!"

I had to roll my eyes when I read the journal entries that said I thought I cared too much to be a nurse—such a hard lesson to learn. Caring without judgment; empathy without control. Although I can start an IV like a pro and am getting better at organizing my shift, the biggest lessons I learned this year were about the boundaries between my patients and me. Respect for the dignity of all patients and family members. Respect for privacy. I can best show how much I care by allowing people to be themselves. I still have to figure out how to do that. I'll admit it here, but never say it out loud. Lots of times, I don't like the way people act toward themselves and other people. Nurses call that being judgmental, and it is a huge no-no. Dad says it's a lifelong job to stop your personal feelings from affecting interactions with people. He still has trouble respecting people who don't live like he thinks they should. He told me that if I could think, analyze, and evaluate, I would be judgmental. The trick is not letting those feelings interfere with personal relationships. We are not God, he said. Let God judge good and evil, and let us be her agent to help. Such a philosopher!

Even Sophia has taught me some things. I still think she talks about social media and her kids too much when she should be in with her patients. *Because of her, I'm more tolerant of difficult colleagues. So. Thanks, Sophia.*

One of my nurse friends at S&S said she writes a list of things she is grateful for in her journal. She looks back at the list and often sees that she could solve a problem better when she needs to. Good idea! So here goes mine for today.

My quilting projects have helped me use my hands instead of my mouth to think through new stuff. Yoga reminds me to breathe, stand tall, and be mindful, not always just busy.

I'm grateful to have been surrounded by those who live empathy, compassion, and respect. That's Barb and Susan and S&S and Amanda and Gram...thanks for the journal, Gram. I didn't get the smartness of that idea either, at first.

I'll stay in nursing for now. I once heard somebody say it was a privilege to care for sick people. I thought that was sappy beyond belief. You know what? Whoever it was, had a point. To be asked to be part of a person's tough times during illness and recovery and even death is an honor. I'm so young. Most of the time, I don't feel like I know enough about nursing, let alone life, yet people much older and wiser have trusted me to care for them and help them. That's weird and cool. And scary.

I applied for an open position on nights on 3 North. Yes, that's right. Nights. Susan is so happy and has promised me that she will make sure I get adjusted. Gram reassured me that I don't have to do nights "forever!" I can use the outstanding night differential pay because things I want and need still seem to take more of my paycheck than I think they should. Now I have a gorgeous apartment where I can sleep without interruption during the day. There is no actual window in that bedroom to remind me whether it is day or night. It turns out that is a good thing, Mom! Nights start on Tuesday, so I better get going. Christmas holiday sales here I come! Later. For sure.

Thank you for reading Kit Wilson, RN, First Year Nurse.

Now I hope you have an idea of what it was like for me and some of my friends as a new RN. This book took a couple of years to write, and a lot has changed.

After residency, I spent a relatively quiet 2019 trying to become more competent in the art and science of nursing. The learning path was uneven, but there was more stability as I got more experience. I continued to learn—a lot.

The night shift did not get the best of me, and 12-hour shifts allowed a pretty normal life. On-call was not the severe impediment to a satisfying life that I had feared.

Making mistakes that could be avoided continues to be my biggest professional fear. Experienced colleagues continued to rescue me when I needed redirection. They hardly ever lost patience with me, and thank heavens my inexperience never got as far as an error.

Nameste. I continued to attend S&S when I wasn't working, and Hannah and I are regulars at yoga. They both helped me keep my own oxygen mask on.

A new group of nurse residents came to the hospital in June 2019, and I saw in them some of the same feelings of shock, confusion, and terror. The new nurses eventually reconciled nursing school practice versus real-life practice in most cases.

The nursing shortage was still felt at TMH, and there is no sign of it lessening. The most experienced nurses are retiring or leaving hospital bedside nursing. It's vital that new graduates feel welcomed and yet keep the care standards high.

My apartment continued to be the best ever. Nothing exciting happened in my family unless you count Maddy and Amanda talking about moving in together and Kai beginning to look at colleges. Gram was counting down the days to retire in June 2022.

In January 2020, I took seven days off and went with Mary and Erin to Miami Beach. We stayed in an all-inclusive resort for sun, fun, and cinnamon rum! While there, we heard about a previously unknown virus that could cause a world-wide pandemic. We had nothing but a historical conception of a pandemic. Pandemics don't happen in modern medicine, right?

Little did we know that this piece of news would control our lives throughout the next two years. If you had told me then that 2020 would be the Year of the Nurse, I couldn't have imagined how fitting that would turn out to be.

In 2020, the nursing profession played a massive role in an enormous culture-changing personal, social, ethical, environmental, and medical breakthrough upheaval. Suddenly the work of nurses and our daily battles for safe and effective health care was front and center. How nurses make some of the madness tolerable for people and share the journey with those faced with the intolerable was becoming better appreciated.

TMH continued to struggle with the issues that blight the health care system in the United States. Things like never having consistently good staffing, not enough money for new equipment, the sickest people being admitted to the hospital, and getting tangled in health insurance issues were not exactly new to me. I entered the new year doing the best I could under these circumstances.

I have more stories to tell you. Some of these stories brought me to tears, some made me snort-laugh, and all of them are worth sharing with those who are nurses and those who are not.

Stay tuned for some wild stories about courage and tragedy, human-kindness, and self-centeredness, as seen through the eyes of a more-experienced-but-nowhere-near-an-expert nurse in the next book, *Kit Wilson, RN, Treading Water.*

About the Author

Beth E. Heinzeroth White

Beth E. Heinzeroth White graduated from a hospital-based diploma school of nursing. She went on to earn Bachelor of Science in Nursing and Master of Science in Nursing degrees. Her career has spanned adult critical care to nursing care of children and perinatal nursing care. She has taught nursing of children and nursing management courses in diploma, ASN, and BSN programs. Beth's clinical practice as a certified Pediatric Clinical Nurse Specialist centered on her particular interests in pediatric palliative care and developmental pediatrics, particularly care of children with spina bifida. She is co-author of two award-winning books: *In the Shadows: How to Care for Your Seriously Ill Adult Child* (2013: Hygeia Press), awarded the 2013 AJN Book of the Year in the Consumer Health category, and *Caps, Capes and Caring: The Legacy of Diploma Nursing Schools in Toledo,* (2018: University of Toledo Press), awarded the Bowling Green State University Libraries CAC 2018 Local History Publication Award in the Independent Scholar category. She is semi-retired and lives in northwest Ohio.

Glossary

The world of nursing is full of words and abbreviations that may be unfamiliar and strange sounding. This alphabetized glossary is meant to help explain some of the medical terms that Kit Wilson, RN, and her colleagues toss around so freely. Every effort has been made to make this list complete and the definitions understandable. We hope it helps.

- o **AAA**
  - Refers to an abdominal aortic aneurysm which is a bulging of the largest artery in the body running from the chest through the abdomen. Rupture of the aorta due to the bulging aneurysm, is life threatening.
- o **Acuity:**
  - Refers to the severity of patients' condition and the level of attention they require from professional staff.
- o **Anisocoria:**
  - Unequal pupil size
- o **Anti-Embolism hose:**
  - Also called TED (thrombo-embolus deterrent) hose. Compression stockings used to prevent blood clots.
- o **Atropine:**
  - A medication with many uses, including increasing a slow heart rate.

o **Arterial Line or Art Line**
  - A catheter inserted into an artery to measure blood pressure more accurately than a cuff.

o **Bilateral**
  - Both sides of the body

o **BP:**
  - Blood Pressure measurement.

o **BSN:**
  - Bachelor of Science in Nursing. A 4-year college degree.

o **Bolus:**
  - A rapid IV injection of a medication. A one-time dose to quickly raise the concentration of a medication in the blood.

o **Cathed or to Catheterize:**
  - To insert a hollow tube called a catheter into an artery, vein, or urethra.

o **Coronary:**
  - Refers to the heart.

o **CABG:**
  - Coronary Artery Bypass Graft. A type of open-heart surgery to treat blocked coronary arteries.

o **Calcium:**
  - A mineral that the body needs for life. It builds bones, enables blood to clot, muscles to contract and the heart to beat.

o **Cannabis:**
  - A plant, also known as marijuana and pot. It may be prescribed for a variety of conditions.

o **Charge Nurse:**
  - An RN who is "in charge" of the unit during a shift. The charge nurse performs the same duties as a staff nurse with some supervisory duties.

o **Circadian Rhythm:**
  - A natural internal 24-hour cycle that regulates when a person feels awake or sleepy.

o **CNA:**
  - A Certified Nursing Assistant has successfully completed a training program learning to help with bedside nursing tasks. This role is called STNA or State Tested Nursing Assistant in some states.

o **CNS:** two meanings depending on the context of the sentence.
  - Clinical Nurse Specialist who is a nurse with advanced education, such as a Master or Doctoral degree in nursing, expert specialty clinical skills, and certification from a national accrediting body. Also known as an Advanced Practice Nurse or APN.
  - Central Nervous System refers to the brain and spinal cord.

o **CPR:**
  - Cardiopulmonary Resuscitation is an emergency procedure that provides chest compressions and ventilation to a person in cardiac arrest.

o **Code Blue:**
  - Code Blue blared across a hospital intercom means an urgent medical emergency. This is usually a patient in cardiac or respiratory arrest.
  - Hospital codes are a quick way to tell hospital workers who need to attend to an emergency. Other hospital codes denote different emergencies, such as a violent person, a tornado spotted, or a hazardous waste spill.

o **Code Brown**
  - A nursing shortcut phrase. It means a call for assistance with a patient care situation where a large amount of feces (poop) is involved.

o **Code Gray**
  - Code Gray blared across a hospital intercom means a need for assistance because of a violent person without a gun.
  - Hospital codes are a quick way to tell hospital workers who need to attend to an emergency. Other hospital codes denote different emergencies, such as an urgent medical emergency, person, a tornado spotted, community disaster, or a hazardous waste spill.

o **Contusion**
  - A bruise in the brain tissue caused by trauma

o **Cranial**
  - Refers to the skull

o **Crash cart**:
  - Also called a Code Cart, it's a red box on wheels with drawers containing equipment and medications for life support in an emergency.

o **CT**
  - Computerized tomography is a specialized x-ray that uses computer processes to create body tissues and bones images. Also called a CAT scan or Computerized Axial Tomography.

o **CVA**
  - Cerebral Vascular Accident or stroke

o **CVL:** two meanings depending on the context of the sentence.
  - Central Venous Line is a long flexible tube inserted into a large artery. Also called Central Line or Central Venous Catheter.

- Cardiovascular Laboratory is a specialty area of the hospital where diagnostic and treatment procedures are performed related to the heart and its associated blood vessels.

o **Defibrillator:**
  - A device used in life-threatening situations to restore a normal heartbeat by sending an electrical pulse or shock to the heart.

o **Dependent edema:**
  - Describes gravity-related swelling in the lower body, such as feet and legs.

o **Diabetes, Insulin-dependent:**
  - Also called Type I Diabetes and is a chronic condition that affects the way the body processes blood sugar. In this form of diabetes, the body produces little or no insulin, so the person needs insulin injections every day to avoid complications. Sometimes this disorder is called by its out-of-date name: Juvenile Diabetes.

o **Diabetes, Non-insulin-dependent:**
  - Also called Type 2 diabetes and is a chronic condition that affects the way the body processes blood sugar. With Type 2 diabetes, the body either doesn't produce enough insulin or resists insulin produced. Oral medications and sometimes insulin are part of the treatment.

o **Diastolic:**
  - The bottom number of a blood pressure reading. Refers to the pressure in arteries when the heart is between beats. In 120/80, 80 is the diastolic measurement.

o **DIC:**
- Disseminated Intravascular Coagulation. A rare and profoundly serious condition causing abnormal clotting and massive bleeding.

o **Diazepam:**
- A controlled medication used to treat anxiety, muscle spasms, and seizures.
- Also commonly called by its brand name, Valium

o **Differential:**
- Refers to the measurement of the types and percentages of different kinds of white blood cells

o **Durable Power of Attorney for Health Care:**
- Durable Power of Attorney for Health Care is a document that lets a person name someone else to make decisions about their health care in case they cannot make those decisions. It gives that person (called your agent) instructions about the kinds of medical treatment you want.

o **Dyspnea:**
- Difficulty breathing.

o **Echo or Echocardiogram:**
- A test using sound waves to diagnose problems with the heart's structures.

o **ED or ER:**
- Abbreviation for Emergency Department or Emergency Room.

o **Edema:**
- Swelling in a body part caused by fluid trapped in body tissues.

o **EHR:**
- Electronic Health Record or computerized patient medical chart.

o **EKG/ECG:**
  - Electrocardiogram, a recording of the electrical signals produced in the heart during the beat or contraction cycle.
  - A 12 lead EKG/ECG looks at the heart's electrical activity from different planes.

o **EMT/EMS:**
  - Emergency Medical Technician, a person certified to perform basic emergency services to ill or injured persons who usually works within the Emergency Medical System, which responds to 911 calls.

o **Epinephrine:**
  - A medication with many uses, especially to increase heart rate, improve breathing and treat allergic reactions.

o **Extubate:**
  - To remove an endotracheal tube which is a catheter introduced to the trachea or windpipe, to maintain a patent airway and ensure adequate oxygen delivery to the body.

o **Femur:**
  - The thigh bone.

o **Fiscal year:**
  - A 12 consecutive month period used for accounting purposes in an organization. A fiscal year may begin in any month during the year and is not always related to the calendar year.

o **Florid:**
  - A deeply flushed or red color of the skin.

o **Foley catheter:**
  - A tube inserted from the outside of the body into the bladder to drain urine into a closed con-

tainer. A Foley catheter has a balloon that helps keep it in place.

o **Fracture:**

- A broken bone.

o **Glasgow Coma Scale:**

- A reliable summary score scale is used to measure a patient's level of consciousness following a brain injury. Scores range from 3 (deep coma or brain dead) to 15 (fully awake.)

o **Graft Occlusion**

- A complication of CABG refers to a blockage of a bypass graft soon following open-heart bypass surgery.

o **Gram negative sepsis or G- Sepsis**

- A systemic infection caused by a specific classification of bacteria that leads to critical illness.

o **Hemorrhage:**

- Refers to very heavy bleeding

o **Heparin:**

- A medication that prevents the formation of blood clots. It may be referred to as a "blood thinner."

o **Hepatitis B:**

- A type of viral infection of the liver caused by exposure to infected blood.

o **HIPAA:**

- The Health Insurance Portability and Accountability Act is a 1996 Federal law that restricts access to individuals' private medical information and limits the amount of health information that can be shared with physicians and nurses who are not directly caring for the person.

o **HIV:**
- Human Immunodeficiency Virus, a virus spread by exposure to infected blood, that attacks the body's immune system and is the cause of AIDS or Acquired Immunodeficiency Syndrome.

o **Holistic Nursing:**
- Based on the understanding that everyone has unique biological, sociological, psychological, and spiritual aspects that fit together to form a whole person.

o **HS:**
- Hour of sleep or bedtime.

o **Hypertension:**
- High blood pressure.

o **I.C.U.:**
- Abbreviation for Intensive Care Unit. A particular hospital unit providing constant expert nursing care, close supervision using life support equipment, and medications to support normal bodily functions. Also known as a critical care unit.

o **Incontinent:**
- Inability to voluntarily control urine and/or feces

o **IV:**
- Intravenous line is a needle or tube inserted into a vein for medication, fluid, or blood administration.

o **Liters per minute**
- A standardized unit measurement of gas flow, such as oxygen

o **Living Will:**
- A living will is a written, legal document that spells out medical treatments you would and

would not want to be used to keep you alive, as well as your preferences for other medical decisions, such as pain management or organ donation.

o **Male pattern baldness:**
  - Baldness on top of the head and front of the head.

o **Maslow's Hierarchy of Needs:**
  - An idea in psychology proposed by Abraham Maslow. Maslow's theory arranges a person's needs and motivations in a hierarchy from basic survival to self-actualization.

o **Medication Reconciliation**
  - Process of ensuring that the patient's medication list is as accurate as possible.

o **MI**
  - Myocardial infarction. A heart attack.

o **MRI**
  - Magnetic Resonance Imaging. A diagnostic test that usesp strong magnetic fields and radio waves to create images of the body's internal structures.

o **Nasal Cannula:**
  - A nasal cannula is a tube or pair of prongs inserted in the nose for oxygen delivery.

o **Nasogastric Tube:**
  - A nasogastric or n/g tube is inserted into the nose, through the esophagus into the stomach to drain fluid or give medicines or nourishment.

o **NCLEX:**
  - The National Council Licensure Examination is a nationwide examination for nurses. Nurses must pass NCLEX to receive a nursing license and practice nursing.

o **NIBP Unit:**
- Non-invasive blood pressure unit is an auto-mated device that measures blood pressure, pulse, and other vital signs.

o **NP:**
- A Nurse Practitioner is a nurse with advanced education, such as a Master's or Doctoral degree in nursing, and a national accrediting body certification. Nurse Practitioners are edu-cated to provide acute, chronic, and specialty care to patients of all ages, depending on their specialty. Also known as an Advanced Practice Nurse or APN.

o **NPO:**
- is short for a Latin phrase to withhold food and fluids; frequently called Nothing by Mouth.

o **O2:**
- Abbreviation for oxygen.

o **OR:**
- Abbreviation for Operating Room.

o **Pain Score**
- Any number of tools that measure a person's perception of pain severity. Scores are often given as a number ranging from 1 (no pain) to 10 (the worst pain you could imagine.)

o **Patient-Controlled Anesthesia or PCA**
- A method of programming IV pain medication so that patients may push a button and self-ad-minister a set amount of pain medication over a set amount of time.

o **PE:**
- Abbreviation for Pulmonary Embolism, a blood or air clot in the lungs.

o **Peripheral pulses**
- Refers to pulses in the arms and legs.

o **PICC:**
- Peripherally Inserted Central Catheter is a long intravenous line used for long-term medications, and blood draws.

o **Platelets:**
- A type of blood cell needed for clotting blood.

o **PPE:**
- Personal Protective Equipment refers to head coverings, goggles, gloves, masks, and protective clothing worn to protect against biohazards and airborne pathogens.

o **Pulse oximetry:**
- Also called Pulse Ox or SpO2, it is a measurement of the amount of oxygen carried in the body's red blood cells and is one indication of the person's oxygen levels in the body.

o **PVC:**
- A Premature Ventricular Contraction is an irregularity of the heart rhythm. The bottom chambers of the heart, the ventricles, beat too early.

o **RN:**
- Registered Nurse.

o **Room air**
- Refers to the percentage of oxygen found in natural air. Room air is 21 percent oxygen.

o **Seizure:**
- Grand mal, also called Tonic Clonic or Generalized, is a type of seizure that involves a loss of consciousness and violent muscle contractions.

o **Senior staff nurse:**
- A designation used to recognize a hospital staff nurse who is not a manager but has the experience and clinical skill that is considered highly proficient, even expert.

o **Sinus Rhythm:**
- A normal regular rhythm of the heart. Also called Normal Sinus Rhythm. If the heart rate is above 100 in an adult, it is called Sinus Tachycardia; if the heart rate is below 60 in an adult, it is called Sinus Bradycardia.

o **STAT:**
- From a Latin phrase meaning Right Away or Without Delay.

o **Systolic:**
- The top number of a blood pressure reading. It refers to the amount of pressure in your arteries during heart contraction. In 120/80, 120 is the systolic measurement.

o **Telemetry:**
- A way to remotely monitor a person's vital signs, such as heart rate, pulse, respirations, and blood pressure. A person wears a telemetry transmitter, and the readings are monitored in another area, such as a nurses' station.

o **TBI**
- Traumatic brain injury. A physical assault or damage to brain tissue.

o **Triage**
- Refers to the sorting and treatment of ill and injured persons based on their severity of illness. Usually, the most serious are treated first.

o **Toxic appendix:**
  - Refers to the appendix's inflammation and infection, which may rupture, spilling infection into the abdominal cavity. This infection can be fatal.
o **Tympanic Membrane**:
  - Refers to the eardrum
o **Type and Cross Match:**
  - Blood typing is the process of determining the blood type and Rh factor of a blood sample. Cross-matching involves finding the best donor for a patient before blood transfusion.
o **Urinalysis:**
  - A diagnostic test that uses several measures to report the number of particles such as sugar, white blood cells, and bacteria in the urine.
o **UTI:**
  - A urinary tract infection.
o **Utilization Management:**
  - A set of evidence-based guidelines that help insurance companies manage health care costs by evaluating in advance the appropriateness of procedures, surgeries, and length of stay in a hospital or extended care facility.
o **Unit of blood:**
  - One unit of whole blood is roughly equivalent to a pint.
o **Ventricle:**
  - A hollow part or cavity in an organ. In the human heart, the bottom chambers of the heart are called the ventricles. The brain also has four ventricles.

o **Ventricular Fibrillation:**
- A life-threatening heart rhythm where the entire heart contracts without coordination so that blood flow to the body essentially stops—usually treated with defibrillation.

o **V-Tach or Ventricular Tachycardia:**
- A life-threatening heart rhythm where the bottom chambers of the heart, the ventricles, beat in a highly rapid and ineffective manner.

o **Vital Signs or Vitals:**
- Measurements that are useful in detecting medical problems. Vitals usually include Blood pressure, Pulse, Respirations, and Body Temperature. Depending on the clinical situation, other Vital Signs may be measured, such as Pain level or Fetal Heart Tones.

o **White Blood Cells**
- The cells in the body which fight various infectious organisms that enter the body and may cause illness.

o **Window:**
- Refers to the length of time between the onset of symptoms and when a patient arrives in the ED and begins life-saving therapy.

Made in the USA
Monee, IL
02 July 2023

38447533R00146